DATE DUE

The Library Store #47-0204

Putting on an Act

by Christi Killien

Houghton Mifflin Company
Boston   1986

Library of Congress Cataloging-in-Publication Data

Killien, Christi.
    Putting on an act.

    Summary: High school sophomore Skeeter McGee is
forced to examine her relationship with her brother,
best friend, and current love interest when a pen pal's
move to town threatens to expose the big lie Skeeter
has told in her letters.
    [1. Interpersonal relations—Fiction]   I. Title.
PZ7.K5564Pu   1986   [Fic]   85-30598
ISBN 0-395-41027-4

Printed in the United States of America

P 10 9 8 7 6 5 4 3 2 1

For my mother and my father, and my own William

1

THESEUS: *Go, Philostrate,*
Stir up the Athenian youth to merriments;
Awake the pert and nimble spirit of mirth.

A Midsummer-Night's Dream,
Act I, sc. i, ll. 12–13

I knew Shag was going to try to sell me something.

He invited me into his bedroom, which he considers his office, and casually asked me how things were going. I said "Fine" and looked around suspiciously for signs of what kind of deal my older brother might be setting up for me, his loving little sister.

But all I saw was the usual stuff. On his desk sat his Konica camera, a bunch of black-and-whites of the last basketball game for the Queen Anne High School newspaper, and his new tripod, folded up. On his bed lay his newspaper collection book and his Safeway bagger apron. He bags groceries there on Mondays, Wednesdays, and Fridays. I can send Shag into a raging fury by merely referring to him as a bag boy; he insists that he is a *man*, and bag man, he says, sounds like a juvenile video game. Or some sort of derelict ne'er-do-well, which is even worse.

On the wall, carefully placed, were his posters, which include the Seattle SuperSonics; an Apple computer advertisement; and, most sacred of all, his poster of Wall Street. You see, Shag's goal in life is to be a millionaire by age twenty-five. After that happens — and he has no doubt that it will — he will live out the rest of his days investing his money and playing golf.

His bookshelf, at first glance, held the usual: spy novels, college catalogues, a stack of *Sports Illustrated* magazines, and a couple of investment manuals.

Then, with a start, I saw *it*. An old, illustrated edition of Shakespeare's play *A Midsummer-Night's Dream*. It looked magnificent. There was a delicate watercolor illustration of the fairy Puck on the cover, gold on the binding, gilt-edged pages, and a gold tassel bookmark, dangling from the bottom. I loved it instantly.

"How much?" I asked brusquely. I wasn't in the mood for games.

"Whatever could you be talking about, Skeeter?" He arched his eyebrows and gazed at me with wide-eyed innocence. Shag even looks like a hustler, with his bright red hair, white eyebrows, and white eyelashes. To me he looks like something that was just dug out of the permafrost.

2

"You know perfectly well what I'm talking about. The copy of *Midsummer's* over there." I pointed.

Shag looked. "Oh. That. Well, now that you mention it, that *is* for sale. If you're interested."

He knew I was *very* interested. Shakespeare is my hero. He is the most romantic man who ever lived.

"I'm interested," I said grimly. If I had been dealing with a normal con man, one who didn't know me so well, I would have feigned disinterest and let him talk me into the book's worth. I'm no dummy. But with Shag I knew I didn't stand a chance. I braced myself for the outrageous price.

"For you, ten bucks."

"Ten bucks! I bet you picked it up at a garage sale for two bucks, max! Forget it!"

"Actually, I got it at Argo Used Books for three-fifty. But I'm sure I can find another buyer, considering your English class is reading this fine play and my particular copy has some excellent notes and comments. Perfect for an essay test."

"I'll give you five," I said, steely-eyed. "Not a penny more."

Shag put on his blithe look. He leaned against his closet door and gazed straight through me as if he were bored to death. And then the merest smirk crossed his face, the kind of smirk that says: I've just amused myself by thinking a vulgar thing about you.

"I forget that you're an unemployed dreamer, Skeeter. I'll keep your *offer* in mind." He said the

3

word "offer" as if he questioned whether or not such a ludicrous amount should even be considered. Shag is a master of intimidation.

Then he added, "Maybe your friend Gena would be interested?"

I just loved the way he slipped that in. He is so disgusting. He's had a crush on Gena Farragut since the beginning of school. It doesn't bother him that she's only in the tenth grade, like me, and that he's a senior. And it doesn't bother him that she barely gives him the time of day. He continues to *accidentally* meet her at her locker or *casually* sit by her at lunch. Talk about obvious. And he doesn't even seem to care.

"Gena Farragut isn't the slightest bit interested in you or your stupid book," I said, glowering, and stomped out of his room.

At least I could be grateful that I didn't have to look at him at dinner. It was Monday, and he was bagging. If I was lucky, I wouldn't have to lay eyes on his slimy dork face for at least another twenty-four hours.

I slammed the door to my room, flopped onto my pink and gray comforter, and hugged my stuffed elephant, Romeo. I felt better already. I could *think* here. My room is so much more civilized than Shag's.

I lay back and glanced over at my poster of William Shakespeare. He looked so serene. "William, life is so miserable!" I cried, and reached for my pen pal Terry's disastrous letter, which lay in the middle of seven crumpled papers on my desk. Seven crumpled attempts at the truth. "I lied to Terry and it's finally caught up with me."

I looked at Terry's even handwriting. "She'll never forgive me, William. And Gena probably won't either because I never told her Terry even existed, not to mention any of the ridiculous lies I've written to Terry."

Shakespeare raised one eyebrow slightly. "I know, I know," I said. "Gena's been my best friend since fourth grade. But she wouldn't understand. And now, when she finds out the truth, Terry will hate me, too." I felt hot tears brimming. "Gena will be here any minute. No more lying for me! Besides, I need her help to get out of this mess."

Gena's prettier than I am, but I'm smarter than Gena. I looked over at my bookshelf to assure myself that, yes, indeed, I really was smart. There were my copies of the classics, *Jane Eyre, Pride and Prejudice, The Complete Plays of William Shakespeare.* Only one other person knew about the books I kept in my closet, buried under a stack of preppie wool sweaters my grandmother always sends me from Boston and which I never wear. Only Terry knows that there lies my special edition book of Charles's and Diana's royal wedding and my Tender Moments and Rapture romances. I bought these books with my own money. I was too embarrassed to check them out at the library.

Being both the serious intellectual type and the

5

sappy closet romantic makes me the way I am, I think: insecure, worried about being discovered as a fake, and often feeling as though I'm putting on an act. I want two things in this world. One is to be a writer. A good writer whom people will respect. And second is to be in love with a very romantic, sensitive guy, like William or one of the heroes in my Tender Moments romances. And, of course, to have my hero feel the same about me.

"Is that too much to ask?" I asked, and then added, "I'm only human."

Shakespeare smiled knowingly. He knew what it was like to be human. He was a poet, and all poets know how humans are miserable about almost everything.

"I mean," I continued, "wasn't it you who said, 'Lord, what fools these mortals be!' right here, in this very play?" I picked up my school folder and plucked out the script of *A Midsummer-Night's Dream*. I was the one who had recommended this particular play to Ms. Masanga, my English teacher, when she asked for suggestions. Unfortunately, I used poor judgment and suggested it during class time, which didn't do much to bolster my popularity.

There was a loud knock on my door. I looked up at William one last time, for moral support, and said, "Come in."

2

THESEUS: *Thanks, good Egeus; what's the news with thee?*

EGEUS: *Full of vexation come I.*

Act I, sc. i, ll. 21–22

Gena's blond hair was piled on top of her head in a graceful chignon. She had just come from her ballet class, and her creamy complexion glowed.

"Hey, Skeeter!" she said, and dropped her quilted bag of ballet junk on the floor. "Hilary called and left your message at the studio, and I came as soon as I could. What happened?" She looked so concerned that I felt kind of stupid for causing so much trouble.

"A mere disaster, Gena," I said, and sighed deeply. "I don't know where to begin."

"This *must* be bad. I've never seen you when you didn't know *exactly* what you wanted to say." Her eyes bored into me, and she sat on the end of my bed, solemn and impatient, waiting for whatever horror I was about to describe.

I was enjoying her concern, I must admit. Usually I was the one with all the answers, the wise, calm one. It felt nice to be the victim, the one with the problem, for a change. "I'm afraid that this might be bigger than the two of us, Gena. It might be out of our hands by now."

"What do you mean by that, Skeeter?" She lowered her voice to a whisper. "You haven't done something *illegal*, have you?"

"You know me better than that," I chided. "I'm too chicken to break the law, anyway. This isn't anything like that. It involves me, and my honor."

Gena thought about that for a moment and then grew quite pale. "Omigod, Skeeter. You're *pregnant?*"

"Shhh!" I was afraid Shag might have heard her. He was still in his room, probably counting his money. Most of his money is in the bank, of course, but he likes to keep twenty dollars or so in his desk, in coins and dollar bills. He likes the feel and smell of it.

"How could you even *suggest* such a thing?" I whispered.

Gena giggled nervously, in a relieved sort of way. "Well, it's not impossible."

"It most certainly is! I've never even kissed a guy. You know that." It was a fact I wasn't exactly thrilled about. Gena kissed a guy, last year at the ninth grade dance, behind the gym. She doesn't talk about it, though. Partly because she doesn't want me to feel bad, partly because she can't stand the guy this year.

"Last time I checked, Skeeter, kissing had nothing to do with getting pregnant." She smiled coyly and started doing some leg stretches.

"This has nothing to do with sex," I said disgustedly.

"Darn." She giggled again. Now she was holding her arms out in front of her and opening them up to the side in the movement she'd told me was *port de bras.* She was off in Ballet Land, and it was my own fault. Nobody likes to play Twenty Questions.

I thought about what there was to like about me as I watched Gena. Surely I had some qualities that Terry could weigh against my chief characteristic: despicable liar.

I'm small and have short, curly brown hair. A Tinkerbell twin, almost. Those are okay characteristics most of the time. I also like my freckles, although I've had to *train* myself psychologically to like them. I did this by deciding that they are little chunks of chocolate that have floated to the surface of my skin, and I *love* chocolate. My favorite sweatshirt of all time is my dark brown one that says CHOCOLATE IS MY LIFE.

"Skeeter? Skeeter, are you all right?" Gena had finished and was staring at me, concerned. "I'm sorry we got sidetracked. I don't know how that happened. Tell me right now what happened today. No more guessing."

"Do you remember Miss Hinky, our eighth grade English teacher?"

"What does she have to do with what happened to you today? Honestly, Skeeter, get to the point!"

"This is important to the story, I promise." I held up two fingers in the Brownie salute and smiled. "Do you remember her?"

"Sure. We used to call her Stinky Hinky, remember?" Gena giggled.

"Yeah." I giggled, too. Miss Hinky sprayed an entire bottle of perfume on herself every morning, leaving a trail of Ambush wherever she went. "Remember when she made each of us write to a kid in that class in Wichita, Kansas? She called it the Pen Pal Project?"

"Yeah," Gena said, frowning. "I wrote to some girl, but never got a letter back."

"Well, I wrote to a girl named Terry. Terry Rothschild Peat. Her father is David Peat, the rich and famous airplane designer." Gena didn't seem terribly impressed, so I continued. "Mr. Peat was in *Time* magazine last month! He helped Boeing design the Seven sixty-seven."

"The only magazines I read are *Glamour* and sometimes *Seventeen*. You know that."

I knew that, and I also knew that Gena wasn't the slightest bit ashamed of it, either. She's not a fake like me. She's always telling me how smart I am, and how she wishes that she knew as much as I do. Can you imagine what she would say if she opened my

10

closet and found such intellectually stimulating books as *Island of Joy, Passion in Paradise,* and *Edge of Temptation*? I shudder to think.

My mother, the English professor, once found *Desire in the Desert* on my bed, where I had carelessly left it. She had shaken her head and said, "Skeeter, how can you abide such shallow fiction? These novels have such inane plots and vapid characters. Surely you can find something more worthy of your time."

"Gee, thanks, Mom," I had said. "I like you, too."

I continued telling Gena my story. "I've been writing to Terry ever since Stinky Hinky's class. We're really good friends now." I paused to see if Gena was going to be stung by my betrayal of our friendship, as I had envisioned her being. Maybe I read too many romances, though, or I hadn't given Gena enough credit, because she didn't even demand a declaration of loyalty.

"And she's been writing you back?" Gena asked, amazed. "That's incredible. I wish someone would write to me like that. I can't even get my dad to write me back."

Gena's dad is still in California, and she's hardly heard from him the entire six years she's lived in Seattle. He's a real jerk.

"Yeah," I said, feeling guilty. "I guess I really should have told you before." I leaned over to the bottom drawer of my desk and carefully lifted the old shoebox, stuffed with letters, onto my bed. The

11

page from *Time* lay on top. "Here are all her letters, if you want to see them."

"Sure." Gena picked up the *Time* page. "He's cute," she said, studying the black hair, aviator glasses, and cleft chin. "Do you have a picture of Terry?"

"No, and I don't want one, either." I wanted to keep Terry in my imagination. I had only a vague idea of what she looked like. Last year she told me that she had gotten a permanent and it made her look like Shirley Temple, and once she mentioned that she hated the volcanic pimples she got every month during her period. But that's all I knew. And I liked it that way. As long as she was still sort of an imaginary person, I could be honest with her about me. Who I really was: the Tender Moments addict who also loved Shakespeare, the sensitive, loving girl who loathed her very own brother, and the intelligent, logical person who was scared to death that her father was going to die from stress and migraine headaches.

I took a deep breath and went on with the horrible rest of it. "Gena, the thing is that I told Terry that I'm very popular at school and that I have a devoted boyfriend." I paused to let that sink in.

"And I just got a letter from her today that says she is moving to Seattle over Christmas, and I don't know what to do!"

Gena stared at me with her mouth agape, incredulous. "Oh, Skeeter," she whispered, "this *is* a disaster. What are you going to do?"

"*I don't know*," I repeated loudly. I could hear a bit of panic rising in my voice. "That's why I need your help."

"I don't understand why you would do such a thing in the first place." Gena was genuinely baffled. She had no idea that I wasn't perfectly satisfied with my life. After all, I'd never even told her about my new and hopeless crush on Campbell Lancaster, my friend since preschool and now the star of the basketball team. Who would have ever dreamed I would fall for a jock? And Campbell, of all people?

"The same reason anyone lies," I said matter-of-factly. "I wanted to impress Terry. I don't exactly lead the most exciting life in the world, you know."

"And who, may I ask, is the lucky guy?" Gena asked with a sly smile.

"Promise not to laugh."

"Promise." She traced a little X on her chest.

"Campbell Lancaster."

"Campbell Lancaster the basketball player?" Gena sounded utterly disbelieving.

"Of course, Campbell Lancaster the basketball player. How many Campbell Lancasters do you know?" I was being sarcastic, I knew, but it was such a dumb question.

"Well, *excuse me*," Gena shot back. "He just doesn't seem like your type."

13

"And what's *my type?* Denny DePew, the two-hundred-pound Baby Huey, or Odie Whipple, the technoid?" Why was I getting so annoyed at Gena's simple question? I looked down, my eyes fixed on the box of Terry's letters.

"*Skeeter.* That's not what I meant, and you know it," Gena said firmly as she looked over at the door, agitated.

"Yeah, I know," I said, feeling contrite. How was Gena supposed to know that Campbell was the man of my dreams, the proverbial boy next door whom I had known all my life and who, in the course of one summer, had been transformed into a tall, incredibly cute hunk with a dazzling smile. Unfortunately, these same qualities had made him an over-the-summer sensation with half the female population at Queen Anne High School.

"I'm sorry I snapped at you," I said. "I just feel so stupid."

"Actually, I'm kind of glad that you finally admitted that you like someone. You never talk about boys."

"Yeah, well, I don't talk about my minuscule bra, either. That doesn't mean that I don't wear one."

Gena laughed. Then she got off the bed, walked over to the door, and, with her hand on the door frame, started flexing and pointing her right toe.

"What's that called?" I asked, as I always ask.

"*Frappé.* It helps me think."

14

"Whatever works." Shakespeare and I watched her, and I knew what he was thinking. Gena had Athenian beauty, just like that of his very own Hermia in A *Midsummer-Night's Dream.*

"I've got it!" Gena cried, turning into a human being again. "It's so obvious. Terry is rich, remember? She'll live in some ritzy area. I doubt if she'll end up on Queen Anne Hill."

Gena had a point. Queen Anne may sound terribly regal, and some very rich people do live on the south side, with sweeping views of Puget Sound and the city, but there were plenty of ritzier neighborhoods in Seattle.

"I'll bet you'll never even see her!" Gena was saying. "In fact, the most you can probably expect is a couple of phone calls. Terry'll get so involved in her new school, she'll forget about you *completely!*" Gena smiled triumphantly.

"Gee, thanks, Gena," I said sarcastically, but then I added, "You're probably right," and tried not to look as devastated as I felt.

"Of course I'm right. Think positively!" She looked toward the door again. She seemed unusually jumpy. "And now I have to go. It's almost four-thirty, and I didn't leave Mom a note." Her mother gets home from work early because she goes to work at the crack of dawn. She's a stockbroker, and *very* strict with Gena and her ten-year-old sister, Hilary.

I watched her gather up her coat and ballet stuff.

15

"I'm going to have to get started on that Shakespeare play tonight," Gena said. "I'll call you if I get stuck, okay?"

"Sure," I said softly, still thinking of Terry's letter.

Shag just happened to be in the hallway when Gena opened the door. He was going to bag in his customary chinos, L. L. Bean shirt, and Top-Siders. Shag is an incurable preppie.

"Leaving?" he queried innocently.

"Yeah."

"I'll walk you. I'm going that direction anyway."

"What a coincidence," I commented acidly from my bed and waved. "Life is just full of little surprises, isn't it?"

"I see you're your usual charming self, Skeeter," Shag replied coolly. "No wonder Gena is leaving."

"You're sure you want to walk with Moneybags McGee, Gena?" I asked with a look of grave concern. "He might try to sell you something."

"Chill out, Egghead," Shag retorted.

Gena shook her head. "You guys. Knock it off." She scowled at me, then turned to Shag. "Okay, Shag. Thanks. It's almost dark out, so I'd like some company. Talk to you later, Skeeter."

"Can you believe him, William?" I asked my mentor when they'd gone. "The unmitigated gall of standing in the hall, waiting for Gena to leave."

Shakespeare agreed.

"Shag's style is so glaringly unromantic. And he

wasn't even embarrassed," I said with disgust.

Shakespeare smiled.

But then, thinking of embarrassment reminded me of the last letter I had sent to Terry.

I had told her all about a date, which I had totally made up, of course, in which Campbell had taken me to a movie and then to McDonald's. McDonald's isn't exactly an enchanting setting, but I had to be realistic. I told her about how I had gotten our order since Campbell was in the rest room. When he came back to the table, I had decided to do an imitation of a McDonald's person, like one I'd read about in *Popularity High*, a Tender Moments romance. I said, "One cheese quarter, two Macs, two fries and a coupla Cokes, sir," and then I stuck a fry in Campbell's mouth. "Taste good?" I asked. He swallowed the fry and said, "It's okay. But this tastes even better." And he had leaned over and kissed me, several times.

I had actually written that to Terry! Pretty far out. But *very* romantic.

"So how am I ever going to explain it, William? Terry will never forget me. I know that. After all, she's written to me for two years! So I've got to come up with something good, and I've got to do it fast."

Shakespeare looked especially grim because he knew the real clincher to this whole mess.

Christmas break was only a week and a half away.

17

3

HELENA: *O, teach me how you look, and with what art You sway the motion of Demetrius' heart.*

HERMIA: *I frown upon him, yet he loves me still.*

Act I, sc. i, ll. 192–194

Some families have severe, dramatic problems. Fortunately, my parents are still married and in love. And I don't think my brother is into drugs, alcohol, or sex. Just money. But we are still screwed up in a normal, undramatic, suburban sort of way.

Take my father. He's a CPA, and he hates it. CPA stands for Certified Public Accountant. He never comes right out and says, "Accounting stinks," but I can tell he feels that way. For instance, he is spending more and more time in the yard, digging, weeding, and moving plants around. He loves to work with plants, and gardening always relaxes him.

Another way I can tell that Dad is sick of his job is by the books he checked out of the library last week: *Practical Formulas for Hobby or Profit, How to Manage Real Estate Successfully — In Your Spare Time,*

18

and *Earning Money Without a Job.* I've found that you can tell a lot about what a person is thinking by what they check out of the library. Obviously Dad wants to quit and make money in some other way. It's part of my theory about why Dad has so many migraine headaches. A job you don't like gives you stress, and stress gives you migraines.

I also noticed Shag looking through *Earning Money Without a Job,* but he's a different case altogether. He gives everybody else stress. Except for Mom. My mother is a combination of me and Shag. She looks more like Shag, with her red hair and bangs, and she has his go-get'em personality, but she went after her Ph.D. in English instead of a million dollars.

Anyway, Mom and I ate dinner alone together because Dad came home with his fourth migraine in three weeks and went immediately up to bed.

"Have you ever told a lie — I mean a really *bad* lie — and been caught in it?" I asked, not looking up. I poked at the bits of potato chip Mom had sprinkled over the top of the tuna casserole.

She thought for a minute and then, looking directly at me with large, questioning eyes, she said, "Yes, I've told a few whoppers in my day. I suppose everybody has."

"Probably." I was trying hard to sound casual. "So, what did you lie about? And what did you do about it? When you were caught, I mean."

"Well, let me see if I can remember the most humiliating one, as I'm sure that's the one you want to hear about. Right?"

"Absolutely."

She made a face and was quiet for a while. Then a devilish grin spread across her face. "I thought of one," she said, "but I'm certainly not very proud of it, Skeeter."

"I can tell," I said. "You look positively penitent."

"Don't be so smart." She sipped her coffee. "My behavior was contemptible, and I'll tell you about it only because it will be a valuable lesson to you."

Mother has always been concerned that our conversations have educational value. We can laugh and joke to a point, but in the final analysis it usually comes down to a lesson.

"Do you remember my ever talking about Alan Hutchins?" She chewed her lip in an effort to hide a grin.

"Sure. He's the real tall guy you dated before you met Dad."

"Right," she said, and reminded me of his more intellectual qualities. "He was a fine poet, Skeeter."

"Right," I echoed, then giggled. "Alan, the tall poet. Dad used to call him Longfellow." I had to admit it was a pretty dumb nickname, really, but Dad made a great face to go with it. He loved to tease Mom about her old boyfriends because it always embarrassed her. She had a lot of them, and, according to Dad, they all could be described with the same set of adjectives. Sort of like the Seven

20

Dwarfs: Ugly, Nerdly, Odd, Abnormal, Eccentric, Irresponsible, and Weird.

Mother chose to ignore my Longfellow remark.

"I was seeing a guy named Jeff when I first met Alan," she explained, and fluffed her bangs with her fingers. "Jeff had asked me to a party. I said no, that I had plans to study with some girlfriends at the library."

"Sounds suspicious to me already," I said.

"I guess it does — now. But then it seemed perfectly reasonable."

"Perfectly reasonable to a lovesick college coed."

Mom smiled and downed the last of her coffee. "I was very studious. Anyway, I lied. I really went to a movie with Alan."

"How did Jeff find out?"

"I'm getting to that part." She frowned. "Unbeknownst to me, there was a fire at the library that night. It broke out in the basement, but the fire department shut down the entire library. The next day, when I saw Jeff, he asked me how my studying went."

"Oh no! What happened? What did you say?" I asked the question, but I already knew the horrible answer.

"I told him that it went fine, that I got a lot of work done. And then he said, 'I suppose the sirens and the fire trucks didn't even bother you.' I said, 'Oh no, we kept our noses to the grindstone the whole night. We didn't even stop for a break.'"

"He tricked you, Mom," I said in summary.

She started laughing.

"What's so funny?"

"I just thought of what I must have looked like when he told me that the library had been closed all evening. Talk about egg on my face!"

"Sort of like that time when I swore to you that I hadn't eaten the chocolate cake, and you reached over and wiped a huge glob of chocolate frosting off my cheek." That had actually happened. And just last year. The only saving grace of the humiliating incident was that Shag hadn't witnessed it. "I was caught red-handed."

Mom laughed again and stood up. She started to clear the dishes. *"In flagrante delicto,"* she said with satisfaction.

"What? What did you say?" Mom loves little foreign phrases. It's a mania that she says is an occupational hazard.

"In flagrante delicto. It's Latin. It means 'while the crime is blazing,' or, as you said, 'caught red-handed.' "

Mom scraped the dishes into the garbage disposal, and I put the milk back in the refrigerator. I didn't feel greatly helped or relieved, but I wasn't blind to the humor of our situations. Only it would have seemed a lot funnier if I wasn't being caught in a blazing crime at that very moment. Mom's confession was slightly comforting, though, just knowing that she had been caught in a humiliating lie and survived.

"Thanks for telling me about your lie, Mom," I said. Then I thought of something. "Hey, did you tell Jeff the truth?"

"Yes, and I'm glad I did."

Here it comes, I thought. The Lesson to Be Learned. The Happy Ending Because the Truth Will Out.

"Jeff had met a girl at the party and really liked her. He didn't know how to tell me that he wanted to see her again, so when I told him the truth about Alan, everything worked out wonderfully." Her assured smile reminded me of Gena's assured smile when she announced a few hours earlier, "Don't worry. Terry'll forget about you *completely!*"

Life wasn't so easy for me. I couldn't just write to Terry and say, "Look I lied to you. Can things still be exactly the way they were?" I couldn't say that because, deep down, I knew things never *would* be the same between us. Once she saw my ordinary face and my average house and met my warthog of a brother, she'd know I was a fake. A fake she would never want as a friend.

Mom looked at me, her eyes level with mine. "Telling the truth is the answer," she said in a mild voice, but I knew it was much more than motherly advice.

"You're right," I said politely, electing not to discuss the matter further. "Thanks again. I've got to go do some reading for school, so I'll see you later."

I knew Mom wanted to hear about my lie. She continued to look straight at me with a sad curiosity on her face. I felt bad about not telling her, but I couldn't. Not yet.

"I'll tell you about it later, Mom," I said, and smiled sheepishly.

"You don't need to, Skeeter." She shook her head. "Just remember what I said, okay?"

"Okay. And thanks for dinner."

I left. It was Mom's night to clean up, and I really did have to get started on *Midsummer's*. I'd read it once, last year, but I'd forgotten a lot of it. It's kind of a complicated story.

I plopped onto my bed and flipped through it, remembering bits and pieces as I flipped.

Two guys, Lysander and Demetrius, and two girls, Hermia and Helena, get all mixed up about who loves whom when a fairy named Puck drops love juice in their eyes. It's pretty bizarre.

Bizarre situations seem to abound in my life lately.

And rereading *Midsummer's* got me to thinking. Gena had been acting awfully mysterious lately. As well as nervous and jumpy. Like the other day, when she was telling me how much she wanted to go to the Christmas dance with a boy.

"Friday. The dance. I wish someone would ask me," she had said, pouting.

"Someone already asked you," I reminded her.

"That doesn't count. You know that Mom would *never* let me go with Roger Patillo. She hasn't met him, and he doesn't exactly make the greatest first impression."

That was true. Roger was into punk rock and had dyed a swatch of his hair green. He wore a studded leather wristband and had a rattlesnake tattooed on his forearm. I imagined Gena's delicate hand resting on Roger's in one of those yucky wedding photographs, the kind meant to show off the lovely couple's rings. No way. Mrs. Farragut would never let Roger through the front door.

"You know, Gena," I had said abruptly, "we can always go without dates. It's not that big of a deal."

"I know," she had said and sighed. "I'd just like to go with a boy, *for once.*"

"Yeah." For a moment I had imagined Campbell cornering me against my locker at school, passion blazing in his eyes, refusing to let me go to class until I agreed to go with him to the dance. I would yield, of course, but not immediately, since I would have already promised another guy that I would go with him.

"Yeah." Gena had sighed again.

I remembered that when Gena was talking, I had the distinct impression that she had a specific someone in mind. And maybe, just maybe, that someone was Campbell.

The phone rang, and I raced down the stairs to see if it was for me. I didn't want Mom to have to come up and get me, and I knew she wouldn't yell since Dad was sick.

"Thanks for coming down," Mom said, smiling, though she still looked concerned. "It's Gena." She handed me the receiver and left, closing the kitchen door behind her. Mom really is pretty understanding. Especially compared to Gena's mother.

Gena and I went through the usual greetings and then I surprised even myself by confronting her with my suspicions. It's amazing how love can drive a person to doubt her own best friend. It happens in Rapture romances all the time.

"Do you *swear*, Gena? You don't like Campbell?"

"Skeeter! I don't like Campbell Lancaster. I swear." She paused, as if reconsidering, then explained. "He has *looked* at me kind of funny, but looking doesn't mean anything. He's never said anything or made any moves. Anyway, now I know *you* like him, and as far as I'm concerned, he's yours."

"Thanks. Now if I can just get *him* to realize that!" I laughed, more from relief than because my joke was so hilarious. Then I decided to change the subject. "Did Shag get you home all right?"

"Ha-ha, very funny. Hey, are you reading *Midsummer's*?" Gena asked, also changing the subject.

"Yeah, but it's kind of complicated."

"I know! I'm still only on the second page. I didn't know the saying 'The course of true love never did run smooth' came from this play."

"Lysander only said that so Hermia wouldn't feel

26

guilty about running off to the woods with him. I think he's a creep." For some reason, Lysander's slick ways reminded me of Shag.

"Maybe," Gena said thoughtfully. "But I feel sorry for him a little bit. He really loves Hermia."

That was interesting. And it made me think of something else.

"How do you know that, Gena?" I hurried to say the words before I lost my nerve. "I mean, how can you tell when a guy really likes you?" I had been curious about that for a long time. According to most of my romances, it's all in the eyes. Passionate, dark, knowing eyes. I hadn't seen any of that kind in the halls of Queen Anne High School.

"I don't know," she said seriously. Then she giggled and added, "But I guess he must love her. He wrote her poetry and sang under her window at night."

I laughed too. "And he gave her sweetmeats. I mean, if a guy gives you sweetmeats, he *must* be serious!"

We both cracked up. Then Gena groaned. I knew she had to go. Mrs. Farragut restricts Gena's phone time. It's a precautionary measure to keep Gena from getting married when she's sixteen, like Mrs. Farragut.

"Look, I've got to hang up," Gena said grumpily. "It's been fifteen minutes. See ya tomorrow, okay?"

"Okay. Bye."

I trudged back up to my room and forced myself

to do my geometry homework. Then, after two unsuccessful attempts to get involved in Hermia's and Lysander's problems, I gave up and got into my pajamas. I snuckered down under my wonderful comforter and hugged Romeo.

"Good night, William," I said tenderly to my poster and snapped off the light by my bed. The last thing I remember was hearing Shag walking down the hall after working at Safeway all evening, jangling the change in his pocket.

4

DEMETRIUS: *I love thee not, therefore pursue me not.*

Act II, sc. i, ll. 188

*T*he next day at school, everybody in English was acting goofy. They had Shakespeare on the brain.

Ms. Masanga took attendance. Then Rob Peters shouted, "Hey! Some fool hath filch'd my pen! 'Twas right here upon my desk!" Everybody laughed.

Then Andy Walvatni said, "You want for your pen, but, forsooth, you never were possessed of one!" Andy looks like Beaver Cleaver with glasses, and he's very funny. He also knows Rob really well. Rob always bums a pen off someone before class starts.

"Pert boy," Rob said. "I will square with thee later."

"Oh, a quarrel! A quarrel! Methinks I fear a quarrel!" That was Melissa Baumgardner. She's a cheerleader and loves to be the center of attention.

"Be advis'd, fair maid, I won't inflict cruel pain."

Rob again. Everybody hooted. "Fair maid" is pretty heavy talk, especially since it is common knowledge that Rob likes Melissa.

"Gentle sweet, you shall see no such thing," Andy said, getting down on one knee. "I — "

"Thank you, thank you," Ms. Masanga cut in. "I'm glad to see that you read your assignment." The class groaned.

"It's hard!" Alan Gates said in a whiny voice. He always whines.

"I know it is," Ms. Masanga said with a fake smile. Ms. Masanga is very dramatic. She is tall and thin, has long black hair, and wears black clothes a lot. She also wears purplish-red lipstick, which exaggerates the two bumps in her top lip. She reminds me of Bullwinkle's arch cartoon villain, Natasha, of Boris and Natasha. I'm always expecting her to say, "Hello, *dah-lings*," in a Russian accent, but of course she never does.

She started reviewing what had happened in the first act, and Gena, who sits two rows over from me, whispered, "Skeeter."

I looked.

She waved a folded paper very discreetly under her desk. A note for me.

Oh, brother. This meant getting Denny DePew's attention. He sits between us, planted there by Ms. Masanga as a block. Literally. Denny weighs at least two hundred pounds. From October through April he has a cold, and snot burbles out of his nose. He has this huge pot belly, and by sixth period, when we have English together, there is a patch of filth on the front of his T-shirt where his belly has brushed against everything in the halls, cafeteria, and rest room. I can always tell what he's had for lunch. For instance, on this particular day I noticed a blotch of dried mashed potato crusted over the little balls of polyester that sprouted from the midriff of his shirt.

Gena slipped him the note, and he slid it up and over the patch and handed it to me.

"Thanks, Denny."

He smiled. Beneath the mess, he's really a pretty nice guy.

After checking it for mashed potato, I opened the note. It was from Campbell to Gena. I recognized his small, tight handwriting instantly.

> Dear Gena,
> I don't know how you feel about me, but I really like you. Do you have a date to the dance next Friday? Would you go with me? I'll call you tonight.
> Campbell

Then, at the bottom of the paper, in Gena's round handwriting:

> I'm sorry, Skeeter. I didn't know, honest. He put this in my locker today. Of course, I won't go with him.

31

I knew it. I just knew it. I glanced over at her. She shrugged and looked extremely forlorn.

I mouthed, "Do you want to go?" I felt mean making her miss out on a date, especially now, since I didn't have a chance of getting Campbell to ask me.

She started writing again. Ms. Masanga was still talking. Denny passed me the note.

> I want to go to the dance, and Mom will let me go with Campbell because she knows him. But I wouldn't feel right. You're my best friend, Skeeter! I don't want you to be mad at me. But believe me, I don't like him. We're just *friends.*

The whole situation was so humiliating. I knew what Gena said about not liking Campbell was probably true. Could she help it if she was gorgeous? I looked over at her and mouthed the single word "go." She still looked miserable, but I felt even more so.

Then Ms. Masanga's voice changed. She was assigning parts to read out loud.

I scrunched down in my seat, which, let me tell you right here and now, is the wrong thing to do if you don't want to be noticed. Ms. Masanga immediately assigned me the part of Helena. And then, cruel fate, she assigned the part of Demetrius, the guy Helena loves, to Campbell. Campbell was excited about it. He loves to read out loud.

The purplish-red lips told us to turn to page nine.

Campbell plunged into his part, reading as though he was Orson Welles or something. He was practically yelling at me: "I love thee not, therefore pursue me not!"

I blanked for a minute, feeling my face growing molten hot. How could this be happening? Then Campbell's voice boomed, reading his last line a second time so I'd wake up: "Hence, get thee gone, and follow me no more!"

I read my line like a robot, quickly and without feeling. From what I could tell, I was essentially saying, "Hey, I love you like crazy and I'll follow you anywhere." How degrading.

It was Campbell's turn again. I only caught his last nine words: "I am sick when I do look on thee."

And then the bell rang. I was first out the door and, fortunately, I didn't start crying until I had made it to the girls' bathroom.

"Are you all right?" It was Gena, looking stricken. She had followed me into the bathroom.

"NO," I said, leaning against the pink tile wall. "Would *you* be all right if the one you love just told you that you make him sick?"

"That was Demetrius talking to Helena."

The bathroom was empty, and Gena placed her hand on the sink and started doing some leg lifts. I

33

don't think she was even aware of what she was doing.

I brushed the tears off my cheeks. "I know. But it sure sounded like Campbell. And it's not just that. Now that Campbell likes you, there's no hope for me, and Terry is going to be here in a week!"

"I already told you that Terry isn't going to be a problem," she said, "and as for Campbell, the way he read those lines, he sounded like a jerk."

"Yeah, I know," I mumbled. Gena didn't understand about Terry, so I stuck to the Campbell complication. "He did kind of overact."

"But you still like him, don't you?" asked Gena in a sympathetic voice, her leg high in the air behind her, bent at an impossible angle.

I nodded miserably.

"I know the feeling." She balanced on one foot for a moment, then she dropped her leg and added quickly, "Look, I'm not going to the dance with Campbell. It's not right. We can go without dates, like we said before."

"No," I said, agonized. "You go with Campbell. I'm so humiliated right now, I don't think I could go with him even if he asked me." That wasn't true, of course.

"Skeeter! He wasn't saying those things to *you!* You've got to remember that!"

I nodded again.

"Come on. Let's go home. The halls are pretty empty now." She pulled on my arm.

34

"Good," I said. "If I ran into Campbell, I'd die."

Gena groaned. "Where's your spunk, Skeeter McGee? If I ran into that big mouth right now, I'd smash his face in."

I smiled. "With your foot, right?"

"A *grand battement* straight to the chops," she said, and laughed.

When I got home, Mom was in an intolerably good mood.

"Hi, sweetie! How did school go today?"

"Don't ask," I said grouchily.

She was frying chicken. The floor next to the stove was covered with newspapers, and Mom had on her raggedyest jeans and an old flannel shirt of Dad's. She wears that shirt whenever she fries something so that when the hot oil spits, she won't get burned.

"Are there any cookies?"

"Oatmeal." She lifted the last piece of chicken out of the skillet, added it to the mound cooling on paper towels, and slid the smoking skillet off the burner.

She turned around and gave me a warning look. "But don't spoil your dinner. I've slaved over Ken for two solid hours."

Ken was her nickname for the Sears Kenmore stove. Mom loves to nickname things. She's the one who gave Shag and me our nicknames. My real name is Keeley Anne McGee. It's Irish. Mom doesn't know why she started calling me Skeeter, except that she thought it was cute. Cute, yes, for a three-year-old. But on the other hand, since I'm not a heck of a lot bigger than that now, I guess Skeeter still suits me.

Shag is really Brian Marshall McGee, Jr. When he was born (I've seen the pictures), he had gobs of shaggy black hair that stuck straight out all over his head, like a dandelion gone to seed. And it did go to seed. After three months, it all fell out.

"And besides all this frying," Mom continued, "I spent the entire morning buried under a stack of freshman papers." If the day had been so rotten, I wondered why she was so cheery. I was definitely picking up positive vibes.

"Chicken looks good." I grinned and got a cookie from the cookie jar.

"Guess what?" She was smiling again. "Remember when you told me about how you think Dad's migraines come from stress over his job? Well, I agree with you."

"You do?"

"Yes," she said firmly. "Your father is under a lot of strain at work. And it's going to get worse after Christmas. It's the end of the year."

"I think he should quit," I said blithely, and bit into the cookie.

Mom sighed and poured herself a cup of coffee. "I do, too."

I couldn't believe my ears. "Really? You want Dad to quit?" I didn't think she was serious; I mean, if she wanted him to quit, he might actually do it. And then what would we live on?

"Don't look so worried! I make enough to support

us. Besides, he'd find something soon. I'm sure of it."
She leaned against the counter and sipped her coffee
thoughtfully.

"Well, maybe. But, Mom —"

"And we do have some savings."

I moaned. The idea of Dad's actually quitting was
scary, even though I really wanted him to. "But
what else could he do?" I asked.

"Lots of things. Your father is a very talented
man." She turned off the fan over Ken. The skillet
had stopped smoking.

"True, but so is Mr. Lancaster. He was unemployed for a *whole year.*"

"Greg Lancaster is a computer programmer, and
he did just fine working at home," she pointed out.
Then she got a weird expression on her face: happy,
but vaguely mischievous. Sort of like the way Shag
looks on payday. She gulped the last of her coffee
while she thought some more. Finally she said, "I've
got to make a phone call."

I poured myself a glass of milk and got another
oatmeal cookie while Mom dialed. She saw me and
whispered, *"No more."*

I nodded solemnly and asked, "Who are you calling?"

But she was already talking. "Annie? It's Maggie.
Hi! How are you feeling? I know! Only one more
month!" Annie Lancaster, Campbell's mom, was
eight months pregnant. She and Mom have been
friends since they met when Campbell and I were in

the same preschool. Sometimes Mom acts so silly about Mrs. Lancaster's baby, you'd think *she* was the one who was pregnant.

"How's the packing coming?" The Lancasters are moving to a larger apartment to make room for the baby. "Ummm. It *is* a lot of work," Mom said, shaking her head.

"Hey, I've got a question for you." She was serious now. "Was Greg eligible for unemployment when he was laid off from Boeing?"

I wondered if Campbell was home from basketball yet, and, if so, if he was listening to his mother talking to mine.

Silence. Then Mom said, "Uh-huh, yeah. Uh-huh."

I sat at the kitchen table nibbling my cookie, trying to figure out what Mom was up to.

"Is it the same if you quit?" Silence. "Oh."

I nibbled faster on my cookie.

"One more question." Out of the corner of my eye, I saw Mom glance at me and lower her voice. "Do you know if John Drosendahl's is still available?" Silence. "Ummm."

John Drosendahls? Who was that? And what did she mean by *available?* I stuffed the rest of the cookie into my mouth.

"Thanks," she said excitedly. "What?" She listened, and then motioned for me to come to the phone. "Sure, Skeeter is right here."

She held the receiver out to me. "Annie is calling

Campbell to the phone. He said he wanted to talk to you."

I shook my head wildly, my mouth crammed full of cookie. Finally I swallowed the humongous mass of oatmeal and raisins. "Tell him I'm not here!"

My mother looked puzzled. "I already told Annie you were here. And besides," she said with a meaningful look, "that would be lying. What's the matter with you, Skeeter?"

"Nothing," I whispered. "I just don't want to talk to Campbell!"

"Why not?" she whispered back.

"MOTHER. Just tell him I'm not here."

"Campbell? Hi! Yes, she's right here." She laid the phone on the table.

Traitor. Dirty traitor. I glared at her.

I briefly considered running away, up to my room, and hiding in my closet. But if I ran away, Mom would be more suspicious than she already was, and she couldn't find out that I liked Campbell romantically. She'd tell Mrs. Lancaster and then it would be all over. I wasn't ready for Campbell to know yet. I had to work the whole Terry mess out first. And, besides, when Campbell did find out, it had certainly better not be from his mother.

Even if my mother promised not to tell, she'd still act weird around Campbell. Probably smiling and winking a lot.

I resolved to be cool and, in an exquisitely composed manner, lifted the receiver off the table. "Hello?"

"Hi, Skeeter! How's it goin'?" He sounded quite enthusiastic.

"Fine," I replied.

"That's great! Hey, you gonna be home tonight?"

"Yeah." I closed my eyes for a minute, tried to relax, and took a deep breath. Campbell actually wanted to come over!

"Good. I wanna ask you something. See ya in about five minutes. Bye!" It took me a lapse of a couple seconds to absorb what he had said.

"Campbell? Campbell!" He had hung up. I couldn't believe it. Hadn't he said *tonight?* Five minutes isn't exactly tonight! Five minutes! FIVE MINUTES AND CAMPBELL WILL BE HERE!

"What was that all about?" Mom asked innocently.

I felt trapped. I wanted to be furious with her for saying I was here, but I couldn't afford the time.

"Are you mad at Campbell?" She looked so sickeningly sincere.

"No, I am not mad at Campbell." I clamped my mouth closed. It's very difficult to remain calm when a traitor acts so completely blameless.

"Well, I'd hardly call 'Fine' and 'Yeah' a conversation between friends." She laughed. "If you're not mad, then why didn't you want to talk to him?"

"*Mother*," I said grimly, "Campbell will be here in five minutes; no, make that four minutes. I am going

40

upstairs now." I stomped out of the kitchen and up the stairs. When I got into my room, I slammed the door and tore through my closet, looking for something decent to wear.

I ended up with my puffed sleeve shirt with the lace collar, the Chocolate sweatshirt, and jeans. I like the way the lace looks against the dark brown. I fluffed my hair and pinched my cheeks, although they were already quite pink. I thought I looked pretty cute. Not like Lady Di, not beautiful or glamorous, but definitely cute. Now, if only Campbell wouldn't mention the incident in English today, I could be on my way to winning his heart away from Gena and having a boyfriend to show Terry.

5

LYSANDER: *I mean, that my heart unto yours is knit*
So that but one heart we can make of it;
Two bosoms interchained with an oath,
So then two bosoms and a single troth.

Act II, sc. ii, ll. 47–50

When the doorbell rang, I raced down the stairs, violating everything I knew of romantic protocol. But I really couldn't make an entrance; this wasn't even a date. I had to maintain perspective.

Campbell looked great. He had on a heavy brown jacket with leather patches on the elbows, slightly faded blue jeans, and hiking boots. His glasses fogged up, and he tripped over the entry mat when I asked him in, but, still, he somehow seemed so handsome.

"Hi!" he said loudly. Loud enough, in fact, for my mother to hear him from the kitchen. She was probably listening for his arrival, anyway.

"Hi, Campbell!" She came through the kitchen door, drying her hands on a towel. "Long time no see!"

Campbell laughed and adjusted his glasses. "Yeah,

42

I guess I haven't been around much. Basketball, ya know." Then he gave her a tolerant, kindly sort of smile. He was almost a foot taller than she.

"You've got to come over more often. I miss seeing you around!" she effervesced. I was afraid she was going to hug him.

I suddenly felt very awkward for Campbell. What if he *purposely* hadn't come over? What about that? What if he had other, more interesting things to do?

Campbell shuffled around and mumbled, "I miss you, too."

Fortunately, Dad saved the day by coming through the back door and yelling from the kitchen, "Anybody home?"

Mom backed into the kitchen to greet him, waving to Campbell. "Talk to you later," she said and was gone. The last I heard was Dad saying, "Boy, it's freezing out there."

"Sorry about Mom," I said. "She can really make a person feel guilty."

Campbell shrugged. "I don't mind. I like your mom." Then he looked at me, right in the eye, and laughed. I knew what he was thinking. The fire in my cheeks was still smoldering from the humiliation two hours before. All I could think of was how Campbell had said, "I love thee not, therefore pursue me not."

"That play is pretty funny, isn't it?"

"Yeah. Funny," I snorted.

And then the conversation stopped. I wanted to

sink through the floor and disappear. Finally, I remembered *his* mother. Mothers seemed to be safe enough conversation.

"So, how is your mother?" I asked politely.

"Fine. She is *gigantic*, though!" He puffed out his cheeks to illustrate. "If you ask me, I'd say that kid is ready to come out!"

I blushed. I didn't want to talk with Campbell about kids coming out, either.

"Hey, Skeeter," he said softly. "I need to ask you something, but it's kind of embarrassing. Can we go someplace private?"

I was stunned. I had rehearsed this scene a thousand times in my mind. I would show Campbell into the living room; he would sit next to me on the couch and clasp my hand in his. He would look longingly into my eyes and say, "Skeeter, I know we've been good friends all these years, but now my feelings for you have changed." Then he would kiss me, tenderly, and ask me to the dance.

But it wasn't to be. Instead, he stared at me for a moment, grinned, and broke my fragile fantasy by saying, loudly, "Hey, Looney Tune! Are you there?"

That brought me back to reality. "Yeah. How about the living room?"

He tossed his jacket on the coffee table, collapsed into Mom's reading chair, and proceeded to tell me what I already knew. That he really liked Gena and had asked her to the dance.

"What I wanted to ask you," he said, leaning

forward and grinning eagerly, "is whether or not Gena likes *me?* You're her best friend. I know she's told you."

I took a deep breath and tried hard to accept this cruel turn of fate while maintaining a calm, harmonious exterior. "Let me put it this way, Campbell," I said slowly. "She doesn't hate your guts."

Campbell laughed and said in a cocky voice, "Come on, Skeeter. What does she *really* think?" He lay back in the chair, his fingers laced together across his stomach, the thumbs sticking up, and I thought of the hand game "Here's the Church." His long legs were sticking out into the middle of the room, crossed at the ankles, one heavy hiking boot lying on top of the other.

I swear, it was the Fonz with glasses.

Little did he know that his dear Gena wanted to smash his face in — I believe those were her exact words — that very afternoon. If he wasn't so cute, and if he didn't have this weird spell on me, I would have told him so. His attitude was definitely starting to bug me.

"I told you —"

But I was interrupted by my mother. She came in, potato peeler in hand, and asked Campbell to stay for dinner. And never mind checking with home; she had already called and it was all right.

Talk about timing! After that conversation, I just wanted Campbell to vanish, vamoose, go away. I needed time to construct a new boyfriend strategy.

45

Or at least to brood over this latest humiliation. Instead, I had to sit across from Campbell for an entire meal. And that wasn't the worst of it.

Campbell followed me into the kitchen and, accidentally, stepped on my heel with his clunky boot. I tripped, vaulted through the doorway, and landed with a thud on the kitchen floor, like a drunken Nadia Comaneci doing her floor exercise. I've got a Nadia body, but not her moves. Shag was sitting at the kitchen table and burst into hideous laughter.

Campbell apologized and offered a hand to help me up, but my dignity had already taken such a beating from him, I couldn't be a good sport anymore. "Move," I said, scowling. "You're in my way."

I quickly assessed the damage: a floor-burned elbow, a bruised hip, and a crushed ego.

Campbell smiled awkwardly and pushed his glasses back. He seemed genuinely sorry until he saw the fried chicken. Then he forgot all about me. "All *right!*" he shouted, just like a true jock. I thought he would slap Mom's palms, but he controlled himself.

Thankfully, I heard Dad on the back porch, and when he came through the door, I wanted to hug him. He had been working in the garage with some hyacinth bulbs, which he was forcing into bloom, and he looked like a kid at Disneyland. He beamed. "I've been playing in the dirt," he said. His hands were black with potting soil, and flecks of vermiculite twinkled in his dark hair, like glitter. A few twinkled on his bald spot, too.

Mom laughed. "Dinner's ready, dear."

Dad hung his grimy work jacket on a hook by the back door, washed his hands, and sat down. A black crescent remained under each of his fingernails.

"Hi, Campbell." Dad passed him the chicken. "How's it going?"

"Great!" Campbell said with beer commercial gusto. He grinned broadly and took the platter of chicken.

It occurred to me that Campbell was louder and more obnoxiously cheerful than I ever remembered his being, and I felt a twinge of disgust. Then I thought, perhaps he's acting this way because he feels *uncomfortable*. He really hasn't been here in a long time, and he's self-conscious. Maybe I should be more understanding.

But my interest in being more understanding, already practically nil after our talk about Gena, faded fast when Campbell and Shag started talking basketball.

SHAG:	So, are you guys ready for Roosevelt next Friday?
CAMPBELL:	We beat 'em last year. Hey, Skeeter, pass the rolls, please.
SHAG:	Who's startin'? Skeeter, pass the salad.
ME:	Please? (I looked at him meaningfully, expecting a little courtesy.)
SHAG:	(With a grotesque puckered face and faked girlish voice.) *Please?*

ME:	Creep.
CAMPBELL:	(Oblivious.) Peters is startin' for sure. And maybe Berkowitz. Maybe me.
SHAG:	Hey, that's great! I heard about your knee. It must be better if you're startin'.
CAMPBELL:	Yeah, it's okay. Just a little stiff. (And then to Mom.) Looks like great chicken, Mrs. M.!
SHAG:	(To Mom, sweetly, with a snide side glance at me.) It's really good, Mom. *Thank you.*
MOM:	(With a glowing smile.) Thank you! Take all you want, Campbell. There's plenty. Skeeter, would you get the butter, please? I forgot it.

After I returned with the butter, I continued to ignore Shag's delighted face as best I could.

SHAG:	*Thank you,* Miss Manners. (Fake smile. And then to Campbell again.) What did you guys do during turnout today?
CAMPBELL:	Ran some lines, then we scrimmaged. The usual stuff.
SHAG:	Yeah. Are you going to the dance after the game?

It was at this point in their excruciatingly boring conversation that I looked down at my plate for the first time. I had been so busy passing bowls and plates and getting the butter, I hadn't noticed that Dad had been serving my food for me. When I looked down, my plate was full. I was so astonished that I announced, just as everybody else started eating, "Hey, I've got two breasts!" Then I realized what I had said. I was mortified. Beyond mortified.

My discovery so startled Campbell, who had been in the middle of a large swallow of milk, that he choked and ran to the kitchen sink, where the milk exploded from his mouth and nose. It was absolutely horrible! A judge would have been hard pressed to determine which of us at the table was redder, or more surprised.

Shag started laughing hysterically, the pig. Mom dashed to the sink, trying to help Campbell clear the milk from his lungs, and Dad, still at the table, grinned and offered to help Mom, but she waved him away. Campbell just needed space to cough and spit. The worst of the attack was over.

Dad poured himself a cup of coffee and started talking. Campbell was recovering nicely, and I think Dad was trying to draw attention away from him. Good ole Dad.

"I got an interesting phone call this afternoon," he said, "from John Drosendahl." Shag had stopped laughing and was stuffing his face.

49

"Oh?" Mom snapped her head around. "What about?" She looked uncomfortable and a little nervous.

"I didn't know you knew who he was," Dad said casually, sipping his coffee.

"Who is he?" I asked suddenly. I remembered Mom's mentioning that name to Campbell's mom earlier, but I had forgotten about it with all the commotion over Campbell's visit.

Mom had asked if he was *available*. What did she mean by that? *Available*. And then, horrified, I realized. It was just how Angelica Fairfield felt in *Hot Paradise Moon* when her terribly rich husband was always away on some business trip. It all fit. Dad unhappy in his work, incapacitated by migraines, Mom restless and ready for love.

"He's a client. I keep his books."

"Is that all?" I sounded like an investigative reporter.

"Yes, that's all." He laughed. "That's what I do for a living, Skeeter. Remember?"

"*Dad.* That's not what I mean." I didn't know how to say it, exactly. "Did he say he was *available* for anything?"

Dad frowned. "I don't understand what you mean."

Mom quickly shut off the water in the sink and hustled Campbell back to the table. "You'll be fine now," she said, patting him on the back. She was definitely behaving suspiciously.

Dad passed the potatoes and smiled. "You'll need lots of energy if you're starting against Roosevelt."

Campbell gave him a sickly grin and took the bowl of potatoes, averting his eyes quickly from the breast still on my plate.

"What did Drohn Josendahl want, dear?" Mom said, and giggled. Now I *knew* she was panic-stricken. Scrambled language is a sure sign. She was trying to cover up her guilt with childish giggles, and I was furious. I didn't care if Campbell *was* there, she wasn't going to get away with it! But just as I was about to demand that she tell all, Dad started talking.

"*Drohn* is going to sell out. He's made his place available for a week now and has a possible buyer. He wants me to show the guy the books."

"What business is he in?" Shag blurted out, suddenly interested.

Dad sighed. "Shag, would you *please* enunciate your words more clearly? And *slow down*."

"O-kay," Shag replied with exaggerated slowness. "What business does he own?"

"Drosendahl's Nursery, over on Sixty-fifth Northeast."

"BABIES?" Shag and I asked in unison.

"No," Dad said. "Plants. He has a fine business, but he wants to retire with his wife to Arizona, where his grandkids are."

"Brian," Mom said tentatively, "maybe *we* could buy the business."

So that's what Mom was up to. She wanted Dad to quit his job and run Drosendahl's Nursery. I swallowed deeply. Mom wasn't looking for another man. What if I had actually said something like, "Admit it, Mom! You are a nymphomaniac chasing men recommended to you by Campbell's pregnant mother." The thought was so gross, so thoroughly horrifying, I shuddered. But I thought buying a nursery was a great idea.

Dad looked amused. "With what? My good looks?"

Campbell laughed but stopped quickly when I glared at him, my eyes narrowed to slits. He had exhausted my love and my patience. I realized that Campbell was not the Tender Moments hero I had wanted him to be.

"I'm serious," Mom said, frowning.

"I am, too." Dad shifted uncomfortably and took his plate to the sink. "Thanks for the delicious dinner, Maggie."

"You hardly ate a thing," she snapped.

"It was perfect." He stood behind her chair and kissed her on the bangs. "I'm just not starting against Roosevelt on Friday." All the *men* laughed.

Mom looked tired and exasperated.

"If you'll excuse me," Dad said, taking his jacket off the hook, "I've got some work to finish in the garage. Nice seeing you again, Campbell. Good luck on Friday!" And he was gone.

The rest of the meal was more basketball talk, a few Safeway anecdotes from Shag, and general gloominess from Mom.

Campbell and Shag managed to eat almost all of the chicken, including one of my breasts. All that was left was a back and two scrawny wings — hardly a decent snack.

Dinner was over. Campbell thanked Mom again, gave me a red-faced smile, and went out with Shag. As they left, I heard Shag ask Campbell whom he was taking to the dance. I didn't hear Campbell's response, which was no great loss. I already knew. And, at this point, I was relieved that Campbell's and my romance had begun and ended all in my head.

Mom and I were alone at the table again.

"I think it's a good idea, Mom," I said heartily. I felt sorry for her.

She gave me an odd, quizzical look. "What is?" She looked really spaced out.

"We should buy that nursery."

She sighed. "Dad'll never take the risk. He's too damn conservative." She shook her head in disgust.

"Don't give up yet." I started to chew my lip as I thought about it. I should take my own advice. Terry wasn't here yet. I had to press on and make sure she didn't find out about Campbell.

Suddenly I realized it was Shag's night to clean up, and I didn't want to be around for him to abuse.

"I'm going upstairs to study," I said. "I'm way behind in my reading." I dashed out of the kitchen and up to the relative safety of my room.

I opened *A Midsummer-Night's Dream*, but my heart wasn't in it. I couldn't get my mind off Terry and what to do about Campbell. I glanced down at the scene I was supposed to be reading, where Lysander is trying to get Hermia to sleep with him.

LYSANDER: One turf shall serve as pillow for us both —
One heart, one bed, two bosoms, and one troth.

Good grief. Two bosoms. The whole miserable dinner episode came crashing back in on me. Could it be that I, Skeeter McGee, actually pointed out to my family, *and to Campbell Lancaster*, that I have two breasts? Incredible, but true. Now I have to live in fear of saying something else to humiliate myself.

I looked back at the play to see how Hermia responded to Lysander's lust.

HERMIA: Nay, good Lysander. For my sake, my dear,
Lie further off yet; do not lie so near.

Good for her. I felt inspired by Hermia's example. Who cared about tonight, anyway? Campbell wasn't exactly super smooth. And Terry would probably

54

never find out about Campbell. Tomorrow was a new day!

Unfortunately, my sudden exhilaration didn't last, for just then I heard Shag coming down the hall. He shouted, "Good night, Dolly Parton!" and slammed the door to his bedroom.

6

HELENA: *O, I am out of breath in this fond chase!*
The more my prayer, the lesser is my grace.

Act II, sc. ii, ll. 88–89

*I*t seems as though the harder I try, the more
thought I put into a problem, the worse it becomes.

Another letter from Terry, this one on yellow stationery, was waiting for me when I got home from
school the next day.

> Dear Skeeter,
>
> I've got *big* news. Dad just got back
> from Seattle. He couldn't find a house so
> fast, but he rented an apartment! I asked
> him to check the name of the school so I
> could ask you about it, and it's Queen
> Anne High School. Isn't that where you
> go?
>
> I hope we have some classes together.

I'd like to try out for the volleyball team, too.

I'll look up your number when I get to Seattle. Dad and I are flying there on the sixteenth. Everything is so hectic here. Dad wants to get moved soon so I can start school right after the break. I'm kind of sad to leave here, but I'm really excited about seeing you, so it's not too bad. See you soon!

Love,
Terry

I shuddered. This letter made it all so real. So inevitable. *So soon.* It was already Friday the eleventh. Only five days before Terry's moving day! And she'd be going to school with me! If she doesn't dump me because I'm a liar, I thought, she's so sophisticated that she'll be popular instantly and will dump me then.

I glanced around my room. Silence. No one was home. Shakespeare stared down at me from the wall, but he was thinking about something else. He really wasn't here, with me.

My room felt cold and ugly, and I noticed all of its faults: the water-stained wall below the window, the repulsive eggplant-colored dresser that was my grandmother's when she was young, and the large, pukey green rug with the Victorian curlicue design.

Several times, during my notorious rearranging fits, I've hauled that monstrous rug down to the basement, vowing never to lay eyes on it again. But the wood floor in my room is very cold and hard without it, and I always end up dragging it back.

Mom promised me a new rug someday, after the entire inside of the house is painted, the backyard fence is finished, and we own a computer. In other words, never. In the meantime, of course, she has a nickname for it. She calls it — ready for this? Ready to be thoroughly offended? — Onus, which she swears is not a part of the human body.

Last spring Mom watched as I angrily wrenched the rolled-up rug through my door and hoisted it over one shoulder. She thought it was great entertainment. "Well, Skeeter," she said, "looks like the onus is on you." Then she burst out laughing.

Later I looked that word up. It means "disagreeable burden." That is an example of my mother's perverted sense of humor. I made her promise never to use that word in front of my friends, or I might do something drastic. She said okay, as long as I don't bug her about the rug. Mothers are experts at deals.

I put the letter safely in the shoebox in my desk drawer and decided to call Gena. I had to talk to someone.

Just as I got to the bottom of the stairs, of all the rotten luck, Shag burst through the front door.

"Skeeter! Just the person I want to talk to!" He

tore off his ski jacket and flung it onto the stairs.

"I don't want to talk to you."

He followed me into the kitchen. "It's about the game next Friday night. I speak as your friend, Skeeter."

I looked at him, rolled my eyes, and got a Chocolate Chip Chewy Granola Bar out of the cabinet. I decided to use the phone in my parents' room. It was just a matter of time before Shag started to tease me about the night before.

"I talked to Mom and Dad, and I can take Odor." Odor is our car, a Toyota. Sometimes a stinky sulfur smell floats into the car and makes us all gag, so Mom took Odor in, but the mechanic said that the smell was the catalytic converter and we were stuck with it. Mom started calling it Toyodor, but now it's plain Odor.

Shag poured himself a glass of milk and took the two leftover chicken wings out of the refrigerator. "I'll give you and Gena a ride to the game, and home after the dance, if you want."

"Gee, thanks, Shag," I said sarcastically. "But Gena's already got a date." I chomped down on the granola bar.

"I know. Campbell told me." He gulped his milk and ignored my tone of voice. "I'm offering a ride."

I tried to figure it out. Mom or Dad must have bribed him. Probably he couldn't have the car if he caused me any more mental anguish. Or maybe they

59

threatened to fine him, or not let him go to work. Whatever it was, it had to do with lust or greed. Of that I was certain.

"Fine," I said. "But I'll have to make sure it's okay with Gena."

"Sure. Whatever." He shrugged and grabbed the chicken wings from the counter. "I've got to go to work. See ya later."

Hilary answered the phone when I called Gena. "Oh, hi, Skeeter! Guess what? I'm doing a book report on *The Black Stallion,* and I'm making a shadow box of the island, and Alex and the Black will be on the beach, and I'm going to use one of the little horses you gave me!" Hilary is in the fifth grade and in love with horses. The only reason she stopped her onslaught of news was because she was out of breath.

"That's great, Hilary," I said quickly. "Is Gena there?"

"Yeah. Hold on. *Ge-na!* Skeeter's on the phone!"

I could hear Mrs. Farragut in the background, telling Hilary to cover the mouthpiece when she called someone to the phone.

"Sorry I yelled, Skeeter," Hilary said. "Here's Gena."

"Hi." It was not a happy hi. "Guess what?" I said.

"You guess what," Gena said. "Campbell Lancaster is a total creep."

"I know, I know. What did he do now?" I had already told Gena at school that I didn't like Campbell anymore; I didn't go into the gory details, though.

"He told Shag that I was crazy about him. And then he said that *I* asked *him* to the dance!"

"Did he tell anybody else that?"

Gena paused to think. "Not that I know of, but he could have. Shag just mentioned it to me after school today. He said that Campbell bragged about it last night after dinner at your house."

"Did you tell him that it wasn't true?" I felt like Mike Wallace on *60 Minutes,* probing for the details.

"No," Gena said firmly. "I mean, it just wouldn't have fit into the conversation." She was strangely defensive.

"Wouldn't have fit into the conversation? What's to fit?"

"Skeeter McGee," Gena said huffily, "it just didn't fit. *Okay?*"

"Okay," I said. I had an ominous feeling about all of this, as if Gena was withholding important information. I decided to try a different tactic and divert her from her after-school conversation.

"I wouldn't worry about it, then," I counseled. "He was kind of embarrassed last night at dinner and was probably trying to look tough to Shag." I liked the way that came out. Now, if Gena was still worried, she'd have to explain why.

But Gena was silent.

"Gena?"

"I'm still here," she said, sounding as though she was the last soul on earth after a nuclear holocaust.

"Gena, what difference does it make? *You* know

you don't like Campbell, right? You're just going to the dance with him to have a date. *Who cares* what he tells my stupid brother?"

"Skeeter," she said softly, "I care."

Oh no, I thought. Please, no. But it all started to add up. Gena's nervous behavior lately, her constant looking at my bedroom door, her excitement about walking home with him. How could I have been so blind?

I looked around to be certain Shag wasn't lingering outside the door. He said he was going to work, but he couldn't be trusted.

"I can't believe it," I whispered into the phone. *"Shag?"*

"Yes, Shag. He's very cute, Skeeter."

"Cute?"

"And not only that, he's interesting."

"Interesting?"

"Yes! And quit repeating everything I say," ordered Gena. "You don't see him like I do. You look at him through tinted glasses."

I thought of something Helena says in *A Midsummer-Night's Dream,* and I recited it to Gena: " 'Love looks not with the eyes, but with the mind, And therefore is winged Cupid painted blind.' "

"I'M NOT BLIND!" Gena roared, *"and this isn't English class."*

"Okay, okay!" I said, and elected to change the subject. "You'll be happy to know that Shag has offered to take us to the game and home from the dance."

"Really?" she said in a feathery voice. "Shag offered to drive us?"

"Yes, really. And Campbell has to be there early, so he'll only be with us for the ride home."

Gena was silent for a moment, probably fantasizing about how glorious the ride would be.

"Hey," she said suddenly, "what happened at dinner last night to embarrass Campbell?"

I had to change the subject, fast. "That's not important," I told her impatiently. "What *is* important is the letter I got from Terry today." I hesitated, trying to decide the best way to handle it. "Can I come over?"

"Sure. I've got to get off the phone, anyway. Mom's giving me her hostile look."

Whew! She had forgotten about her question, thank heavens.

"And be sure to bring Terry's letter."

I told her I was on my way. I went back to my room for my Nikes and Terry's letter, wrote Mom a note saying where I was, put it on the kitchen table, and left.

The walk to Gena's was very refreshing. I had on my blue parka, with the hood up, because it was drizzling. Gena says that the blue really accentuates my eyes.

I stuffed my hands in my pockets and felt the cold

wetness on my face. The streetlights were on, and the Christmas lights on several houses radiated bright Life Saver colors through the misty darkness.

It didn't seem like Christmas to me yet. Gena and I had tried to get into the spirit by going to the Northgate Mall the previous weekend. We each bought an Orange Julius and walked, slurping, over to the large, roped-off North Pole area, run by elves who looked more like *Playboy* bunnies, in their red velvet and white fur.

We watched a terrified child getting his picture taken on Santa's lap, his mother promising him a candy bar, a train, and a pony — in that order — if he would just smile. As we left, I made a mental note never to do that to my child. I find myself making notes like that a lot at shopping malls.

Now I walked on down the wet street toward Gena's, wondering what to get my family for Christmas. An impoverished kid like me can't even afford the customary necktie these days. I thought I'd probably get Dad gardening gloves. He goes through a pair every couple of months. And Mom really liked the mittens I bought myself last month. I could get her a pair of those. Gloves and mittens. A theme to my Christmas giving.

And Shag. I'd probably do what I did the year before and just give him the money I'd planned to spend on him. He always takes whatever I get him back, anyway, for the refund.

A bus roared by, full of exhausted-looking people

going home from work, all reading newspapers or staring blankly out into the blackness. I watched the bus stop near the top of the hill, across from the Safeway store where my brother was making his first million.

It still seemed inconceivable that Gena could actually like Shag. I mean, it's like that famous romance about the Beauty and the Beast all over again.

I arrived at Gena's house, and she opened the door even before I could knock. "I was watching for you," she said.

I wondered how many times she had watched for Shag walking by on his way to work. I pictured her gracefully leaping to the window at about four-thirty Mondays, Wednesdays, and Fridays, concealing herself behind the curtains, all in order to watch ugly Shag McGee strut by. It was truly inconceivable.

"Hi," I said, and shook my head. "I still can't believe it."

"Believe it," Gena said as she hung my wet parka on the hall closet doorknob.

Mrs. Farragut was curled up on the cream-colored corduroy couch in the living room, reading the *Wall Street Journal*. She was still in her work clothes: a deep purple silk blouse with a bow, a charcoal tweed skirt, and tiny gold earrings. Her dark brown hair was swept away from her face in thick, permanent waves. Gena told me that she pays seventy dollars every six weeks to have it styled that way.

"Hello, Skeeter," she said and smiled graciously. "Gena tells me that a long-time pen pal of yours is moving to Seattle. The daughter of David Peat."

"Yes," I said, and scowled at Gena.

"How nice," Mrs. Farragut said. "You must want to meet her very badly."

"I do," I said tight-lipped.

Mrs. Farragut looked at me a little oddly. I guess my "I do" sounded about as enthusiastic as a vow taken at a shotgun wedding. There was an uncomfortable silence.

"Skeeter is a little nervous about it," Gena explained suddenly. "Let's go on up to my room, Skeeter. See ya later, Mom."

Gena jogged up the stairs ahead of me, tiptoed quietly past Hilary's closed bedroom door, then closed her own bedroom door behind us and flopped onto one of her twin beds. Her flop onto the bed was elegant. Mine was not.

"Don't say it," she said. "I had to tell her. She heard me on the phone telling you to bring Terry's letter. She wanted to know who Terry was."

"Your mother is too nosy," I said angrily. "Honestly. It's none of her business."

"I know, but she doesn't think it's being noisy. She would say" — here Gena made a face and imitated her mother's voice — " 'I'm just *interested* in your life and in your friends.' " Gena stared up at the ceiling and added hotly, "And *then* she would ask *me* why *I'm* being so defensive!"

66

I felt sorry for Gena. Her mother was impossible sometimes. She twisted things around so much, it was hard to remember what the issue was in the first place.

One time when I was over at their house, there were dirty breakfast and snack dishes in the kitchen when Mrs. Farragut got home. She is a real neatnik, and she yelled at Gena and Hilary, not for being lazy, but for being inconsiderate of *her* feelings. She said that if they really cared about her, they wouldn't forget about the dishes. Talk about a guilt trip. The place is always spotless.

She pouts, too. One weekend when I came over to get Gena to go shopping, Hilary wasn't there. She had gone to a friend's birthday slumber party, and she'd also been invited to go see the play *A Christmas Carol* with the birthday girl that afternoon. Mrs. Farragut didn't have anything to do. Gena asked her if she wanted to come with us, but she made a big deal about how we probably really didn't want her to come.

Which we didn't. Mainly because she was being such a baby. I don't know how Gena stands it.

"Do you want to know what I think?" I said.

"Not really. But go ahead." She rolled her eyes as if to say "Here she goes again, Skeeter the shrink," but from the way she looked at me afterward, with an I'll-try-anything sort of expression, I could tell she really wanted to know.

"I think your mother is very unhappy with her

67

life. She's bored. If she had some interesting things going on in her own life, she'd ease up on you and Hilary. When was the last time she had a date?"

"About a year ago, I think," Gena answered. "Remember that guy she met when she decided to take those golf lessons?"

I remembered. He had told Gena's mother, right in front of Gena and Hilary, that he really liked her swing. Then he gave her mother a goo-goo eyes sort of look. Mrs. Farragut isn't a very good judge of men because she agreed to go out with him once, to Ray's Boathouse for drinks and a salmon dinner. Gena hadn't seen or heard of him since. She understood that to mean that he was mainly interested in a different kind of swinging.

"See what I mean. All she ever does is work. No wonder she's such a grouch. Tonight is Friday night. What is she doing?"

"The same thing she does every other night. Read the paper, cook dinner, work on something from the office, watch a little TV."

"That's the problem, then. She's having romance trouble."

"Aren't we all," Gena said, frowning.

Suddenly I remembered why I had come over in the first place. I dug Terry's letter out of the back pocket of my jeans and tossed it over to Gena. She lay back on her bed and opened the letter.

Gena read. "This is really getting hairy," she muttered. "*Really* hairy."

"What kind of a thing is that to say? *What am I going to do?*"

Gena turned the letter over in her hands and thought. And thought some more.

Finally she said, "There's only one thing you can do if you don't want to tell Terry the truth."

"What? What one thing? What do I have to do?"

"You have to level with Campbell. Make a deal with him. You've been friends with him for years. I bet he'd do it for you. No sweat."

No sweat for Campbell, maybe. But from where I sat, there was plenty of sweat.

7

HELENA: *Wherefore was I to this keen mockery born?*

Act II, sc. ii, ll. 123

When you are desperate, you'll do just about anything. Roger Patillo, the punker who asked Gena to
the dance, had been truly desperate two weeks before in Math. If he screwed up one more time, Mr.
Hansom was personally going to see to it that he was
suspended. But, Roger had told the whole school, if
he made it until Christmas without getting into
trouble, his dad was going to buy him a motorcycle.
Personally, I think his father should have his head ex-
amined.

Anyway, Roger was chewing tobacco in math
class. There it was, bulging under his lip, and he spat
vile brown juice into a paper cup whenever Mr.
Hansom wasn't looking.

Roger sits in the back of the room next to Melissa
Baumgardner, the cheerleader. She saw him spit,

70

and shouted, "GROSS! Roger, you are *so gross!*" which, naturally, got Mr. Hansom's attention off the Pythagorean theorem and on to Roger Patillo.

"What seems to be the problem back there?" Mr. Hansom asked, steely-eyed. He has short gray hair and always wears short-sleeved white shirts, even in the winter. He used to be in the Navy. "Patillo?"

And then Roger did it. An act of desperation. He *swallowed* that wad of tobacco, juice and all. He gagged ever so slightly, then said, with a sneer, "I didn't do nuthin'."

"Melissa?" The steely eyes grew a little less steely.

"I'm sorry, Mr. Hansom. It was nothing." She opened her eyes very wide.

"Pay attention, then," Mr. Hansom said. "This is going to be on the test Friday."

He turned back to the blackboard, and Roger sank back in his chair, his legs crossed and a droll grin on his lips. He looked like the Pink Panther. Until he threw up.

Sometimes situations are so grave, so hopeless, that a person is driven to the Last Resort. We've all been there.

Shag was so desperate to drive Gena to the dance that he gave up the opportunity of a lifetime to tease me.

Gena wanted a date to the dance so badly that she consented to go with Campbell Lancaster, who's a jerk.

My very own father was so desperate to provide for his family that he stayed in a job he hated and endured migraine headaches.

Desperation can drive you to take any risk.

Keep that in mind, because this is my way of explaining why I took Gena's advice and went over to Campbell's right after school. I had stewed over the problem all weekend, and this was the only way. Terry would be in town any minute!

"Sure!" said Campbell after I asked him if he would do me a favor. "Name it."

"Well," I said, fidgeting with a twig I had picked up on my way to the Lancasters' apartment. "It's kind of a long story."

"Walk to Safeway with me, then," he said. "I gotta get some stuff for dinner." He went to get the grocery list from the refrigerator, dodging boxes all the way. The Lancasters' apartment was really small. They did practically everything in that one room, including eat and watch TV. Mrs. Lancaster had turned the eating area into her studio. She's an artist. And Mr. Lancaster's computer was in their bedroom. They hadn't seemed to mind the cramped space. I know I couldn't have lived like that, though. I'd probably have killed Shag.

"We're almost finished packing!" Campbell shouted. The Lancasters had waited so long to move because they wanted to get into this new building, which I hadn't seen, but which Campbell thought was nothing short of the Taj Mahal. It has a pool and a sauna.

"Where's your mom?" I asked. "Is she okay?"

"Oh, yeah. She's at the doctor. The baby dropped this weekend." Campbell locked the door behind us and started down the hall toward the stairs.

"Dropped? Where?" I stopped suddenly and thought, Oh, no. Miscarriage.

"In her uterus, stupid." He laughed and then got very serious. "The baby has changed position. Its head is in the opening of the cervix now, ready to be born."

He looked down at me matter-of-factly, and I willed myself not to blush.

People are so funny. How can Campbell be so straightforward about the *cervix*, and have lost it completely when I mentioned breasts?

He bounded down the stairs in front of me, out onto the sidewalk, and set an Olympic pace with his long stride. He was so absorbed in his description of the dilation of the cervix, contractions, and how his mother's water would break, it was difficult to interrupt him.

But I was breathless. "Slow down," I said, panting, "or I'm going to have a heart attack."

"Sorry, Little One," he said in a sickening John Wayne imitation. "Didn't mean to tucker you out."

"Gee, thanks." I could see now that Campbell had a fully developed tumid head. That's my mother's term for someone she thinks is conceited. I looked up "tumid," and it means "swollen or bulging."

I thought of how Shakespeare put someone just like Campbell in *A Midsummer-Night's Dream*. His name is Bottom. Bottom has a terribly tumescent head, and, as a joke, Puck turns Bottom into an ass. William even called him an ass-head!

"What was the favor you wanted?" said the ass-head.

"It has to do with a friend of mine." I panted for a few seconds.

"Gena?" he said, grinning arrogantly.

"No, not Gena. And, if you don't mind, I don't want to discuss Gena Farragut with you anymore."

"Whoa! Take it easy!" Campbell said, shielding his face with his hands. "Protect me from the wrath of a woman!"

How is it possible, I wondered, to fall out of love so fast? Now my only wish was to punch him in the arm and tell him to buzz off. Unfortunately, I needed Campbell's/Bottom's cooperation.

So I ignored his comment and explained the whole thing to him. Everything from Stinky Hinky's Pen Pal Project to Terry's latest letter. I even told him that Gena knew the whole story and that I would be forever in his debt if he would act like my boyfriend.

After he had a hearty laugh, he ogled me and said, "You really told Terry that I was your boyfriend?"

"Yes. It was temporary insanity."

"Could I get the position full time if I do a good job?" he asked with a smirk.

"Knock it off, Campbell, or I'm going to punch you out."

He did an oh-I'm-so-scared routine and laughed.

"Will you do it?"

"Sure. We go back a long way," he said magnanimously. "I'll consider it a challenge."

"Thanks."

"Oh, I don't have to be your boyfriend at school, too, do I?" He looked stricken. That would definitely cramp his style.

"No," I assured him. "Just around family and family friends. By the time Christmas break is over, we can arrange a fight and be officially broken up."

"Got it, Lover," he said, and burst out laughing again.

We had arrived at Safeway, and as we walked in, I was surprised he managed to fit his gloating head through the door.

It was Tuesday, so Shag wasn't there, but the store was busy. Lots of working people getting food for dinner.

I followed Campbell around as he collected tomatoes, salad oil, rice, and paper towels. "Now for the hamburger," Campbell said, and rubbed his hands together with carnivorous relish. "The *real* food." There was no way I could keep up with his stride as he raced to the meat counter, so I took my time, examining all the new breakfast cereals.

I found Campbell at the steak section and had to redirect his attention. "Come on, Campbell. I don't want to be here all night," I said as I hauled him down to the hamburger. "Hurry up."

All of a sudden Campbell reached over and put his arm around me, yanking me to his side. When I glared at him, he nodded toward the pork section. "Over there," he whispered. "It's Mrs. Farragut."

Sure enough, there she was in her plum-colored coat and boots, studying the pork chops. She really was very attractive.

I cringed. Being close to Campbell did not feel the way I had imagined it would. All I wanted was for him to get his clammy paw off me.

"Get your clammy paw off me," I said.

"Skeeter, Mrs. Farragut is a family friend, remember?" Malicious delight dripped from his lips.

"Holding hands is good enough," I said.

Campbell obliged and rummaged awkwardly through the pile of hamburger packages with his free hand.

I turned my attention back to Mrs. Farragut. A slimy-looking guy had sidled up to her and was making conversation. I couldn't hear what he was saying, but from his slicked-back blond hair and white patent leather loafers, I suspected he was another swinging single type. A weasel with a classic dirty smile.

Poor Mrs. Farragut, I thought. She's had so little

experience with men. She's going to allow herself to be picked up by that scuzz. For all I knew, he could be a rapist.

The same thing had happened to poor Angelica Fairfield in *Hot Paradise Moon.* Before she was married to her creepy husband, she had been very much like Mrs. Farragut — beautiful, well-off, trusting. Too trusting. Her husband was a fiend!

"Do you think this will be enough, Skeeter?" Campbell asked, holding a huge package of hamburger in my face.

"For what?" I asked, distracted.

"Hamburgers tonight. I like at least four."

"Four! Good grief, Campbell. What will your parents eat?"

He laughed and said, "Let's go get some buns."

"Not yet," I said. The leech was still hanging on to Mrs. Farragut. I would have to help her shake that guy! I owed Gena that much. "Let's go say hi to Mrs. Farragut."

"Huh?"

I dragged him over. "Hi, Mrs. Farragut! Nice to see you!"

She looked up and smiled. "Why, hello, Skeeter." Then she saw my hand entwined in Campbell's and looked puzzled. "And hello to you, too, Campbell," she said stiffly. Gena would have to explain to her later, I knew, why Campbell was taking her to the dance and not me. This was getting awfully complicated.

The weasel ogled Mrs. Farragut as she was talking, undressing her with his eyes.

"Gee, Mrs. Farragut, how's little Hilary?" I asked in a loud voice. I was trying to play up her matronly side.

"Little Hilary is fine," she said, looking still more puzzled.

My technique wasn't working. I'd have to try a more drastic approach. "Good. Oh, are you still dating that Seehawk linebacker?"

"What? Skeeter, are you feeling all right, dear?"

"Yes, yes, I feel *fine*," I said exaggeratedly, as I gave a furtive glance over at the weasel, trying to clue Mrs. Farragut in on my intentions. But she wasn't to be helped.

"Oh, excuse me," she said. "I've been terribly rude. Let me introduce you to Jim Cheevers. Jim is the minister at the Pilgrim Baptist Church. He and I were just talking about the youth retreat this spring. Perhaps you'd be interested, Skeeter?"

I groaned silently. The weasel/rapist was a minister! I wanted to die. My mind was really being warped by those romances. "Oh, well, uh, it's good to meet you, Mr. Cheevers. Maybe we can talk about it some other time. But now Campbell has to get home with this hamburger. Right, Campbell?"

"Huh?"

"It was very nice to meet you, uh, sir, and we'll be seeing you, Mrs. Farragut. Let's get going, Campbell," I said through clenched teeth.

"But what about the buns?" Campbell whined.

"We can pick up the buns on the way out." I felt their bewildered stares on my back all the way down the cereal aisle as I whisked Campbell off to the bakery.

"I didn't know Mrs. Farragut was dating a Seahawk!" Campbell said, impressed. "Which one?"

"She isn't dating a Seahawk, Campbell. Which buns do you want?"

"But you said . . ."

"Don't worry about it, Campbell. Just grab some buns and let's get out of here!"

"You really want me to?" Campbell said with a leer, looking down at my rear end.

"CAMPBELL LANCASTER, DON'T YOU EVER LOOK AT ME THAT WAY AGAIN."

"But you're my girl . . ." His voice trailed off as I grabbed a package of buns, marched him to the front of the store, and shoved him into the Express Lane to pay.

"Hey!" he protested. "I wanted to check out the doughnuts."

"Some other time," I snapped. Campbell paid, and I bought a Hershey's Big Block, to calm my nerves. I wondered if this misery was typical of a person whose dream was supposedly coming true. If so, I prefer my old, simpler life, when I just fantasized with my Raptures and Tender Moments.

8

DEMETRIUS: *O, how ripe in show*
Thy lips, those kissing cherries, tempting grow!

Act III, sc. ii, ll. 139–140

*C*ampbell was mine to show to Terry, it was true, but I was beginning to wonder if I could endure his affection over the entire Christmas break, much less put on a believable act for Terry.

Mom asked me to take a casserole over to the Lancasters' after school a couple of days after the Safeway episode. They were finally in their new apartment, and Mom knew Mrs. Lancaster didn't have time to cook. I had to agree to play delivery person since I didn't want to arouse any more suspicion about my troubles with Campbell.

Campbell had agreed to meet me in front of their new apartment building, Mom said, to show me the way.

"Great," I replied, and took the address from her.

Campbell was waiting for me on the sidewalk when I arrived.

"Hi," I muttered.

"Hi, honey!" he said, and reached for my hand. I shook it away.

"Let's not overdo it," I said grimly.

"You're the boss," Campbell said, smiling. I wished he'd quit being so happy.

"Look, like I said, you don't have to be my boyfriend until Terry is around, okay? I don't want Shag or my mother finding out about it yet."

"I'm agreeable. But I'm beginning to like this job," he said, and laughed wickedly. "I hope I can control myself."

"Can it, Campbell," I said. He grinned and pointed at his new building.

"Our apartment is on the fourth floor," he said, looking at the very large, very ugly, ultramodern building, which appeared to be all glass and grayish-green plaster. It looked like a giant slug.

"Doesn't it look kind of *extraterrestrial?*" Campbell said, and he appeared to be having a Close Encounter or something.

"That's a good word for it."

We stood like statues on the sidewalk, shivering and staring up at the concrete growth. The streetlights came on.

"So let's go in, already! It's freezing out here."

Just then a guy passed us and headed up the walk

81

leading to the building's main door. He was carrying a sack of groceries.

"Hi, Campbell," the boy said, and walked back toward us. "I didn't recognize you in the dark."

Campbell forced himself to return to earth. "Oh, hey! How's it goin'?"

"Not bad. We're supposed to get our stuff this weekend. That is, if the moving van makes it over the mountains."

The guy was very, very cute. Critically cute. He was as tall as Campbell and had black hair and dimples. I've only read one gothic romance, and even *I* have to admit, it was pretty stupid. But, I swear, the man in that book, Rafe Dashwood, looked exactly like this guy standing in front of me.

I wished Campbell would introduce us. But he was so into impressing Rafe, he seemed to have forgotten that I was there.

"Yep," Campbell said, stretching. "Unpacking gets old fast, especially if you've got a workout or a game the next day."

I was totally embarrassed. Rafe grinned at me, as if to say "Isn't this guy unbelievable?"

Finally, Campbell remembered me. "Oh, this is Skeeter. She's an old friend. Skeeter, this is Pete."

At last, a name. Pete. I wanted to say two things: "Pete what?" and "Where have you been hiding?"

Pete and I nodded politely to each other and said hi.

"Hey, Pete," Campbell said, "I've got a game tomorrow. Queen Anne's playin' Roosevelt. Why don't you come? We're gonna kill 'em!"

"Thanks. Maybe I will." Pete smiled again and looked at me. "Are you going?"

"Me?" I responded, startled.

"Yes, you. Are you going to the game?"

"Yes," I said, gathering my wits. And then I said a remarkably bold thing. "And you should come to the dance afterward, too. It'll be more fun than the game."

"Well, I don't know about that," the Tumid Head said smugly, and he went through the motions of shooting a basket. He looked like an absolute baboon.

"I'll be there," Pete said, ignoring Campbell.

I couldn't stand the thought of being with Campbell another second, and things were at a nice stopping point with Pete.

"Listen, Campbell, I just remembered. I've got to cook dinner. Mom's got a late class tonight." That was a huge lie, of course, because Mom was home when I left for Campbell's. She had made the casserole.

"Nice to meet you, Pete." I turned and handed the casserole to Campbell and jogged down the block toward home.

After dinner, in the living room, Mom and Dad were arguing. A lot of people would laugh and say, "You call *that* arguing? You don't know what arguing is. They're just *discussing*." But for my parents this was not a discussion. It was a genuine argument.

It was their tone of voice. That was what brought me to the door of the kitchen, where I was cleaning up, in order to eavesdrop.

MOM: Honestly! You are so *tight*, Brian. All you ever talk about is *security!* I don't want to hear that word again!

DAD: Will you lower your voice, please? (A pause.) If by tight you mean that I don't go chasing after every harebrained idea, you're right.

MOM: (Loud whisper.) HAREBRAINED? What, may I ask, is so harebrained about buying a well-established business?

DAD: Nothing. Nothing at all. *If* you have the money. We don't have the money, Margaret. (He calls her Margaret only in the gravest of situations.)

MOM: We have plenty of money in savings, and we could take out a second mortgage on the house.

DAD: (Heavy sigh.) First of all, I've never even *worked* in a nursery. What makes you so sure that I won't run the business into the ground in the first year?

MOM: Don't be ridiculous. That man has a full staff of qualified people, and you've kept his books in perfect order for years. (Mom was definitely winning.)

DAD: There's a lot more to actually running a business than keeping books. I like working with plants, Maggie. But knowing how to pot a primrose doesn't qualify me to manage people!

MOM: I'm *sick* of hearing you underestimate yourself. You can do anything you put your mind to.

DAD: That's shallow, psychological hogwash. I've got to think about *reality*.

MOM: HOGWASH! *Reality!* Let me tell you —

DAD: Yes, reality. Like the reality that Shag will be going to college next year. How can we afford to send him if we use all of our savings on a nursery business?

MOM: (Sarcastic.) Shag can go to the University. He will get some tuition credit because I work there, remember? (Silence for a long minute. I felt miserable.)

DAD: (Softly.) Please don't talk like that. It kills me when you're sarcastic. (Then another, shorter silence.) Shag has been looking into all those colleges in other states. Don't you want to send him where he can get the best possible education?

MOM: The University has an excellent business school, which is what Shag wants. (Then, in a desperate voice.) How much is Harvard going to mean to him if his father is killing himself to send him there!

I couldn't listen anymore. I felt so helpless. I wanted to crawl into my closet and cry, to rock myself back and forth and cry all the problems away.

But I had to finish *my* reality, the dishes. So I stood at the sink and scrubbed, and thought, and scrubbed until they were done.

After that, I didn't know what I wanted to do. I was in a funk. I wanted to go for a walk, but I didn't want to go anywhere. I wanted to watch TV, but I didn't want to watch anything. I wanted to visit with someone, but I didn't want to talk. I ended up going to my room, shutting the door, and sulking.

I had too many problems. Even Mom was worried that Dad might die from the stress. Campbell was a painful disappointment, and Terry might be here in Seattle at that very minute. It was just a matter of time before she called.

My hand mirror, which was lying on my dresser, caught my attention. The mirror side was facing up, and the light reflected off it. I went over and held the mirror under my eyes, with the mirror facing the big mirror on the wall. I looked at all the Skeeters that went on and on forever, deep into the mirror. Somewhere, I thought, deep in the mirror, at the farthest image, is the real me. At the end of the mirrors is the person who thinks back at my reflection.

I tried for a long time to get a glimpse of that person, but I couldn't hold the mirror still enough or at the right angle. All of a sudden, I realized how stupid I must look, holding the mirror up to my face, backward. Maybe I'm crazy, I thought. Maybe I'm losing touch with reality. Or maybe it's just hormones. Whatever, I'd better stop since Shag is home, and he could come barging in at any minute. I don't trust him to knock.

"Shakespeare," I said wistfully, "how is this all going to end? Everything is heading for disaster."

Shakespeare stared down at me, a glimmer in one eye, as if to say "Alas, is this truly such a tortured hour?"

"Well, I guess one good thing has happened," I said grudgingly. "I met a new man of my dreams." I had a few pleasant thoughts about Pete, and then lifted my copy of *Midsummer's* from my desk.

I turned to where I had left off. A kissing scene. Demetrius called Helena's lips "kissing cherries."

I looked at myself in the mirror and puckered my lips, to see how I would look kissing Pete.

"Kissing cherries, William. You said it. So now, Master of Romance, help me win Pete's heart tomorrow night at the game."

William smiled. I was sure he was saying, "I shall anoint young Pete's eyes, and the next thing he espies will be fair Lady Skeeter."

I was absolutely sure that's what he would have said if he could.

9

HELENA: *O spite! O hell! I see you all are bent*
        To set against me for your merriment.

Act III, sc. ii, ll. 145–146

Dad was up early on Friday morning. He said he had a pile of audits on his desk at work and he had to get an early start on them.

An audit isn't an obnoxious little insect, but it sounds as if it should be, right in there with crickets, hornets, and those repulsive fly eggs, maggots. I could certainly understand why Dad didn't look terribly excited about going in to face them.

I wasn't terribly excited about being up, either. I had to bake cookies for the Christmas party in English class, and since I had wanted to get out of the kitchen as quickly as possible the night before, that meant creating two dozen pecan sandies at five-thirty in the morning.

"You're going to Campbell's game tonight, aren't you?" Dad sipped coffee between bites of cereal.

I recoiled. "If you mean the Queen Anne–Roosevelt game, yes, I am."

"I see," Dad said with a knowing look, a look that meant that Mom had told him I had a mad crush on Campbell.

"What do you mean by that?" I challenged. "What exactly do you see?"

"Nothing." He grinned and sipped his coffee again. "Who are you going with?"

"No one." I started to stack the sugar-powdered cookies in an old shoebox. "I'm a free agent."

His forehead wrinkled into deep lines of concern. "You aren't even planning to meet some girlfriends?"

"Dad," I said, annoyed. My stubborn streak reared its determined head and wiped out my insecurities about the evening. "I can take care of myself. I don't need a babysitter."

"I didn't mean that, Skeeter," Dad said, getting a little irritated himself. "But I don't like the idea of your going alone. All kinds of crazies hang around high schools these days."

"Like me?" Shag said, strolling into the kitchen, a huge grin plastered on his face. He had just returned from his morning paper route. "Good morning, Dad, Skeeter. What's all this about crazies?"

"No one asked you to butt in," I snapped.

"Shag, are you going to the game tonight?" Dad said.

"Yeah. I'm taking the car, remember?" For a moment, Shag's light flickered as he waited for a confirming nod from Dad.

"Okay. That's right," Dad said as he took his bowl to the sink.

"And I'm taking Skeeter and Gena," Shag added, his glow returning. "Campbell has to go early to warm up."

"You're not *taking* me," I protested. "You're merely providing transportation."

"Well, madam, your *transportation* leaves here at *exactly* seven-ten. I got my hours changed, so I'm off at six-thirty. Tell Gena we'll pick her up at exactly seven-fifteen. I'm shooting this game, and I can't be late." As if I didn't know that he was taking pictures of the game. He always takes pictures for the paper, and he's always on time.

"Don't worry about me," I said, firing meaningful looks at both of them. "I can take care of myself."

"I'll see you both before you leave tonight," Dad said, looking relieved, and he glanced at his watch. "I've got to get going or I'll miss my bus."

After Dad left, Shag had the temerity to turn to me and say smugly, "I only had your best interests at heart." Then he poured himself a glass of orange juice.

"Bull," I said angrily. "That'll be the day."

"Look, I heard Dad get on your case about going to the game alone, and I came to your rescue. It's as simple as that. Okay?"

"*Nothing,* I repeat *nothing,* is as simple as that

with you," I retorted. "I'm sure there will be a price tag on your gallantry."

"Oh, really, Smart Ass. You think you know me so well," he said with lifted eyebrows. He sipped his juice. "Don't be so sure."

"*You* don't be so sure. And don't do me any more favors, Tightwad." I glared at him with all my strength and without even blinking added, "As I said before, I can take care of myself."

"Right," he said, and laughed. "Just be ready at seven-ten."

He left the kitchen, carrying his stupid glass of juice, and headed up the stairs.

I wanted to scream at the top of my lungs, but Mom was still asleep, and besides, that's not my style.

Instead I finished packing the cookies and thought about how rotten I felt. I hadn't awakened feeling grumpy. On the contrary, I woke up in the delicious warmth of my comforter and moved about quietly, as is my custom, taking my shower and getting dressed. To me, everything about the early morning hours is fragile. Talking, if unavoidable, should be done in whispers; walking should be done slowly and, if possible, in stocking feet; and strenuous thinking or decision making must be kept to an absolute minimum, perhaps to the level of musing or pondering. It was in this delicate state that I was forced to tangle not only with pecan sandies, but also with that rattlesnake Shag, who had bolted out of bed the instant his radio alarm burst forth with the loudest rock band, bounded out into the elements and into the car, with the same obnoxious music blasting, to deliver the morning papers. I felt emotionally ravaged, and I hadn't even been to school yet.

Mom wasn't up when I left the house, hugging my cookies underneath my parka. It was a raw, rainy day, the kind of December day for which Seattle is famous. I wondered what Terry thought of it, since she surely was in town by now.

Tom Pugnetti, Shag's friend, stopped by to pick him up for school in his souped-up 1974 Dodge. Tom asked me if I wanted a ride, too, but I trusted his driving about as much as I trusted Shag's benevolence.

Gena was already at the bus stop when I got there.

"Lovely day," I said, my breath billowing in the cold air.

"You said it," Gena said with her teeth chattering. "I called you yesterday after ballet. Did Shag tell you?"

"Of course not," I replied, and I made up a silly poem to lighten my mood:

What can you expect from Greedy McGee?
He won't take a message without charging a fee!

"I didn't leave any message, Skeeter," she said defensively.

She wasn't amused, and I couldn't think of anything to say about Shag that wasn't derogatory. I was thankful the bus roared up at just that moment, and we climbed in silently. When we were seated in our favorite place — third seat from the back — our hoods off, and our bags and cookies carefully stowed, I was finally able to pry my mind off Shag.

"I wasn't home yesterday afternoon because I went over to Campbell's. I can't believe I actually asked him to be my boyfriend." As I said the words, I realized what I had asked Campbell to be. "Gena, Campbell is my gigolo!" I was aghast.

Gena giggled. "That's not exactly true," she said with a little smile. "He's just supposed to *act* like your boyfriend."

"Well, I don't know if I can stand it much longer, act or not."

"But what will you do about Terry, then?"

"I don't know. I can't think about that anymore. I'm totally *burned out* thinking about it."

"Yeah, you need a rest," Gena said.

We sat glumly, listening to the rain hitting the fogged-up window, and considered that fact. And then I remembered *him.*

"Hey," I said, grabbing Gena's arm. "Are you ready for this? I'm in love again."

Gena grinned. "For someone who has just gotten interested in boys, you sure are off to a flying start."

"It's pent-up passion," I said dryly. "I can't control myself."

93

Gena tossed her head back and laughed. "Who is it this time?" she said. "Not another jock, I hope."

"Nope. He's a tall, dark, handsome stranger named Pete. He's just moved into the same apartment building as Campbell, but I don't think Campbell will be a bad influence on him. He seems to have a mind of his own."

"You've had a chance to check out his mind, too?" Gena said. "My, you *have* been busy since we last talked."

She shot me a sly, suggestive smile, and I had to laugh. "Actually, if you must know, he might be coming to the dance tonight."

We rang the bell for our stop, and Gena shook her head as she bent over to grab her bag. "I have to hand it to you, Skeeter," she said. "You work fast."

"I know." I wedged into the aisle behind Gena. "Making up for lost time."

The day went fairly fast. Since it was the last day before Christmas break, we didn't do much in class. All except for Math. Mr. Hansom gave us a gigantic test in order to, in his words, "keep us on our toes."

Finally it was the last period of the day. English, and Ms. Masanga. Because Ms. Masanga looks as mean and forbidding as a flamenco dancer, stomping around the room in her high-heeled boots and glaring at us from dark, heavily made-up eyes, I was surprised when she turned out to be a real party hound. She even had on a Santa hat.

"Okay, you guys, be quiet," she said, shutting the

door. Her purplish-red lips clashed with the hat. "Finish reading A *Midsummer-Night's Dream* over the break, and then we'll read specific scenes in class when we get back. For today, put all the food on my desk and keep the noise down."

Everybody cheered and headed for Ms. Masanga's desk. She turned on a radio and opened some tubs of dip.

Gena was sitting quietly at her desk with a very unpartylike expression on her face. I moved to the seat in front of hers, since its owner was munching out in the front of the room.

"What's the matter?" I asked.

"Do you really want to know?"

"Of course. What's wrong?"

"I haven't seen Shag all day. He never came to my locker, and he didn't sit with me at lunch. I don't think he likes me anymore."

"Gena, he's crazy about you! He's probably been busy setting up stuff for the dance, or something. You know he's always doing stuff like that."

"Yeah, I guess so." She didn't seem encouraged, so I tried again.

"He was even thinking of you this morning before school."

Gena brightened. "Really? How do you know?"

"He told me to tell you that we'd pick you up at *exactly* seven-fifteen."

She looked disappointed. "That's all? That's what you call thinking about me? Come on, Skeeter. He

95

talks about me like I was a two-minute egg, or something!"

Just then Campbell sauntered over with a pretzel hanging out of his mouth like a cigarette. "Howdy, kiddo," he said to Gena. "Ready for tonight?"

Gena rolled her eyes. "I suppose so" was all she said.

Campbell crunched his pretzel. "I'm really up for the game! Be sure to get there on time."

Gena glared at him, and I think she would have lost control if I hadn't intervened.

"Hey, Campbell, remember that Shag doesn't know about our little arrangement, yet, okay?"

"Gotcha," he said, winking, and poked his finger into my shoulder.

"GROSS!" Melissa Baumgardner shrieked from the other side of the room, where she was giggling with a bunch of her snotty friends. She was all decked out in her cheerleading outfit for the game. I had a brief but horrifying vision of Melissa's group laughing at me, once Terry told them about my bogus Tender Moments dates with Campbell.

Campbell, Gena, and I looked over at her. "Oh, *gross!*" she cried again, popping her gum.

"Hey, keep it down over there," Campbell scolded in an imitation teacher voice. "Didn't you hear what Ms. Masanga said?"

Melissa gave him a coquettish look and mimicked him, saying, "*You* pipe down, Campbell Lancaster," and then broke out in another round of hysterical giggles.

Campbell chuckled indulgently. "I'll see you guys later," he said to us. Then he headed over to that neurotic cheerleader and her friends.

"Have you decided what you're wearing tonight?" Gena asked.

I was too startled to respond immediately. It was the sort of question I expected to hear from Melissa. "What's to decide?" I said finally, and made an unwise attempt at levity. "I'd planned on wearing clothes."

Gena glowered at me. "I'm serious, Skeeter. If you really want to impress this Pete guy you told me about, you've got to wear something besides jeans and a sweatshirt."

"I refuse to dress up in some preppie costume," I said firmly. "There's nothing wrong with jeans."

"No, and you look good in them, but they aren't right for tonight. You've got lots of great clothes that you never wear. I'm coming over after ballet, and we'll figure something out." She smiled a knowing, self-confident smile.

I couldn't think of anything in my closet that could possibly qualify as great clothes. "Just as long as you don't exhume any of the argyle Shetland sweaters."

"I promise," she said, sounding satisfied.

"How about something to eat?" I was eyeing the

97

spread on Ms. Masanga's desk, some heavily frosted brownies in particular. Andy Walvatni, the kid who looks like a Beaver Cleaver clone, was, at that very moment, sinking his teeth into one of those brownies with a look of intense pleasure. Almost as though he was kissing it, or something. Andy is a chocolate fiend, like me.

"You go ahead. I'm on a diet."

"It should be a crime to have as much will power as you do," I said and headed for the brownies. It is beyond me how any sane teenager can survive on a diet of fresh vegetables and yogurt.

Mom was sitting at the kitchen table behind a stack of papers when I got home. She grunted an acknowledgment to my greeting and continued to read. I hunted through the cabinets for the box of Chocolate Chip Chewy Granola Bars, but I hunted in vain.

"Shag ate the last one yesterday," Mom said, not even looking up. It is an amazing and scary fact of life that mothers know some of the thoughts and intentions of their children as well as the children themselves do.

I cursed under my breath and got an apple out of the refrigerator.

Mom leaned back in her chair and paper-clipped the pile of essays. "There was a letter for you," she said, looking puzzled. "But it wasn't sent through the mail. It just has your name on the envelope."

My stomach lurched. I knew it was from Terry. Who else ever wrote to me? And if it wasn't mailed, I thought, that meant it was hand-delivered. She must have brought it in person!

10

DEMETRIUS: *Thou runn'st before me, shifting every place,*
And dar'st not stand, nor look me in the face.

Act III, sc. ii, ll. 423–424

I rushed into the entry hall and pawed through the stack of bills and advertisements. There it was — a lavender envelope with the single word SKEETER on the front in Terry's handwriting. I raced up to my room — apple in one hand, letter in the other — to read and contemplate in peace.

Dear Skeeter,
I'm here! I came by this morning, but no one was home. I guess you'd already left for school. I can't come by this afternoon, so please call me! My phone number is 627–8447.
Love,
Terry

My mind was racing. She had actually been here!

"Oh, William! I'm going to have to face her very soon!"

Mom knocked and I told her to come in. "Who were you talking to?" she asked, looking around the room. "I heard voices."

"No one. Just myself." I bit into my apple and started to hum a little tune. "I was singing, too. Maybe that's what you heard."

"Oh," she said, unconvinced. "Was that letter from your pen pal, Terry? I thought I recognized her handwriting."

"Yeah," I mumbled. "Terry lives in Seattle now. She and her dad just moved here. She left her phone number."

"You don't sound very excited about it."

"I liked *writing* to her, Mother," I explained. "It's not going to be the same talking to her in real life."

"I see." She looked at me suspiciously. "Does this have anything to do with your question about lies, Skeeter?"

"Sort of" was all I said. I had decided long ago that Mom was too involved with the Lancasters to act properly ignorant. And now that I couldn't stand Campbell's guts, I was glad I didn't have to explain *that* to her, too.

When I didn't elaborate, she gave up and got to the purpose for her trip upstairs. "I've decided to have the Lancasters over for a Christmas dinner party on Sunday night," she announced cheerfully.

101

"It's short notice, but between moving and being so pregnant, Annie won't be able to roast a turkey. I was wondering if you'd like to ask Gena and her mother and sister. They don't have any family in Seattle, do they?"

"No. Gena's father is in California, and so are her grandparents." I took another bite of apple and folded Terry's letter. "I'll ask her."

"Why don't you ask Terry and her parents, too?" she suggested brightly.

"Oh, I don't — "

"They're new in town and would probably love a home-cooked turkey dinner." She smiled warmly. One thing I can say for Mom, she doesn't have any trouble getting into the Christmas spirit.

"It's just Terry and her dad," I explained. "Her parents got a divorce last year, and Terry doesn't get along with her mother."

"Terry and her father, then!"

I smiled back wanly. "I'll call her," I said in a thin voice.

"Great! Tell her the time is Sunday at five. Now I've got a lot of planning to do!" she said, and bustled out of my room.

How could I have allowed myself to be railroaded like that? I wondered. I've lost complete control of my life, and it has run amuck. In two days, Terry and Campbell will be here in this very house, exchanging stories about me.

"Tell me what to do, William!" I wailed in desperation.

He looked down at me with the sweet, clear face of reason. "Summon forth Terry and her father as you swore you would," the face said.

I used the phone on the table next to Mom's and Dad's bed and turned my back to the large mirror on the opposite wall. I couldn't look at myself when I talked to Terry for the first time.

"Hello?" I said nervously. "Is Terry there?"

"No," a deep voice responded. "Can I take a message?"

What a stroke of luck, I thought. I'll invite Mr. Peat and not have to talk to Terry until Sunday.

"This is Skeeter McGee. I'm a friend of Terry's."

"Oh, yes. I've seen your letters in the mail."

"Right," I said hastily. "Well, you and Terry are invited to dinner here Sunday night, if you can make it."

"Sunday? That would be fine. It's certainly thoughtful of you to have us over." His voice was very deep and very handsome, and I could almost see his cleft chin.

"My mother is roasting a turkey and inviting a few other friends, too. Would five o'clock be all right?"

"Fine. And can we bring anything? A bottle of wine, perhaps?"

"If you want to, but it's not necessary." That was a dumb thing to say, but it was already said.

"Fine. And Terry has the address, of course, so we'll see you at five."

Fine, I thought as I hung up. A fine mess. I felt like the exhausted fox in a fox hunt, and the dogs were closing in fast.

When Gena arrived, I scrambled to hide the Rapture romance that I had tried to escape into after talking to Terry's father. Unfortunately, I couldn't concentrate, and I doubted whether *Tangled Lies* would have afforded me much comfort, anyway.

Gena was in a much better mood. Her cheeks glowed, and after she tossed her bag on the floor, she struck various poses reminiscent of the prima ballerina Anna Pavlova.

"I'm glad to see that you've recovered, Sugar Plum Fairy," I said, and shoved the romance novel farther underneath my pillow.

"Anthony promised me a leading role in the spring performance!" Her eyes gleamed. "I can't believe it!"

"I can." I sighed and clenched my fists together. Things were certainly par for the course. The fairies of the world were tripping over each other in order to minister to Gena's every wish, trampling over me in the process. "You're not only beautiful, you're also a great dancer," I said.

Gena blushed and adjusted her flawless chignon. "Thanks," she said. "But I'm not a *great* dancer, Skeeter. I've got a long way to go. Thanks for saying it, though."

I thought for a moment. "Yeah, I guess Mikhail Baryshnikov will just have to wait for a couple more years."

She giggled. "At least."

"In the meantime, you'll have to content yourself with Campbell and Shag and the nine million other guys who are in love with you."

"*Please,*" Gena pleaded. "Don't remind me of that jerk. I don't think I can be civil to him for an entire night."

"You might not have to be," I said mysteriously.

"What does that mean?"

"It means that Campbell might end up with a certain cheerleader tonight, and you can be with my darling brother."

"Melissa?" she said, incredulous.

"You saw her flirting with him today between mouthfuls of pecan sandies."

Gena nodded, remembering.

"They deserve each other." I snorted.

Gena laughed. "I hope you're right," she said. "Hey, is that another letter from Terry?" The letter was still on my desk.

"The moment of truth is getting closer," I said, and handed her the letter.

Gena opened her eyes wide in apprehension and read. When she finished she shook her head. "You just missed her, Skeeter."

"I know," I grumbled. "But I won't miss her Sunday. She and her father are coming over for dinner."

"You called her!" Gena exclaimed.

"Yeah, but she wasn't there. I talked to her father. But there's something else. Something far worse." I paused for dramatic effect. "The Lancasters are coming, too."

"Oh, no!"

"Oh, *yes*. And you, Hilary, and your mom are invited also. You're going to have to help me get through this, Gena," I said, feeling utterly desperate.

"I will," she assured me, patting my hand. Then she glanced over to my closet. "And I'm going to start right now." She pranced over to the closet and flung the door open.

"Do you still have those black corduroy pants?" she asked, sliding hangers back and forth on the rack. I felt a little anxious about her being so close to my romances, but they were well hidden. "You know," she added, "the ones you got last Christmas. With the gold belt."

I knew. I'd never worn them because they reminded me of the skin-tights that Roger Patillo wore. He complemented his with black army boots and leather armbands.

Gena found the pants and an old cowboy shirt that my uncle Mike had sent me from Houston. It was a pink and white plaid with sparkling gold threads running through the plaid. I almost barfed when I first laid eyes on it, as country and western isn't my style. Country and western wasn't my uncle Mike's style, either, until he moved to Houston, and, as my dad puts it, became a good ole boy. Now he even wears a hat.

When Gena was finished outfitting me, the only item I had on that I would have deigned to wear voluntarily was my black velveteen vest, which I got at a garage sale because it's funky. Gena had even detoured by her house on her way to ballet and now produced makeup, which she persuaded me to let her apply.

After she was completely finished, I stared at the small person in the mirror. I had on my black cotton Mary Janes, the black pants and gold belt, the black velveteen vest over the gold-accented plaid shirt, a gold metal hairband from Gena, and a face that was actually pretty. Gena had rubbed rouge on my cheeks, applied Desert Sand eye shadow and mascara to my eyes, and smoothed shimmery gloss on my lips. I was the same Skeeter McGee, but a much more sophisticated version.

"You look wonderful," Gena said proudly. "Petite and original, which is what you are."

This time I was the one doing the blushing. "Thank you, Gena," I murmured.

After Gena left, things got quite hectic. Dad came home with another migraine, and Mom was rushing around fixing dinner with a guilty look on her face. I think she was afraid the fight over the nursery caused this headache.

Shag blew in at quarter to seven, wolfed a hamburger in thirty seconds, and charged upstairs to get ready. His parting words were: "I'm leaving in *ten minutes* — with or without you!"

"You'd better hurry up, then," I answered calmly.

"You look very nice tonight, Skeeter," Mom said. She arranged my curls around the gold band.

"Gena did it," I said, and laughed. "I didn't think I'd ever consent to wearing this shirt."

"The whole outfit really suits you," Mom replied.

I rolled my eyes. "Ha-ha, very funny pun," I said, but Mom didn't even realize she'd made a dumb joke. She was lost in her worry.

Shag reappeared in a gray-and-green-striped rugby shirt and chinos. We left, but he didn't speak until we pulled up at Gena's. He turned off the ignition, breaking with his customary honk, and blurted out, "I'll get her."

Gena looked classy in her tweed skirt, oversized burgundy sweater, and brown boots. Shag opened the car door for her, surprising both her and me. I had slipped into the back seat, so Gena slid into the front. Her curled hair swirled around her shoulders, her eyes sparkled, and I thought she would break into a chorus of "You Light Up My Life."

"You ladies look lovely," Shag said, and started the car.

"Thank you, Shag." Gena beamed. "You look nice, too."

It was so obvious that they were in love. I remembered my question to Gena about how she knew when a guy really liked her, and now I knew the answer. It doesn't have anything to do with serenading or sweetmeats. The guy magically becomes a gentleman.

For the rest of the ride to school Shag made similar polite comments, inquiring about our comfort with regard to temperature, music selection, and legroom.

The school parking lot was jammed and it had started to drizzle, so Shag dropped us off at the gym while he went to park Odor. He said he'd see us later at the dance since he had to take pictures during the game.

I've been in the gym a hundred million times, but it was truly transformed on basketball game nights. The presence of parents and little brothers and sisters was an obvious difference. The whole place pulsated with the band's version of "Star Wars" and the warm-up exercises of the players from both teams. It was warm and bright and full of excitement.

Gena and I found seats near the top of the bleachers, and I immediately spotted Campbell, number 18, shooting baskets on the court below with the other players. Melissa Baumgardner was in her usual place, in front of the bleachers, with her white gloves, blue pompoms, and pink cheeks. Either it had escaped her notice that the game hadn't started or she didn't even care, because she was already cheering and yelling like crazy.

Coach Dailey, decked out in a navy sport coat, clapped, and the team hustled over for a final conference. All of the team, that is, except Campbell. Campbell took a detour by the cheerleaders, stopping to murmur some critical message to Melissa before he returned to the pack. Melissa burst out laughing, and Coach Dailey glared at Campbell.

"Did you see that?" Gena uttered a short, sharp laugh. "The two-timing louse."

"Yes, I saw it," I remarked. "That's Bully Bottom for you."

"Huh?" Gena said. "Is that Shakespeare *again?*"

"Yeah! Doesn't it fit Campbell perfectly!"

Gena made an extremely nerdly face at me and looked back down toward the court.

Just then Mr. Hansom, who runs the official clock with its obnoxious buzzer, gave the final signal to end the warm-up period. The student announcer welcomed everyone and led us in the Pledge. I noticed Shag down on the floor with his camera around his neck, his hand across his heart, his eyes on Gena.

When all the opening ceremonies were finished, the game started, and I blocked out everything that was going on down on the court. I wasn't the slightest bit interested in the game. I was looking for Pete.

Gena kept her attention on the court, but she was more intent on watching Shag taking pictures than on the basketball players shooting baskets. Rarely were her eyes on the same general area as the ball.

I searched every bleacher in a logical, sequential manner for most of the game, despite the distractions of all the spectators' comings and goings, and I was sure Pete wasn't there. I felt profoundly disappointed; the entire evening was a waste. I had sat through three quarters of a boring basketball game, looking absolutely sensational, for nothing.

Then he walked into the gym. He walked slowly, his hands in his pockets, taking it all in. I watched as he began to study the bleachers.

"There he is!" I shrieked, jabbing Gena with my elbow.

"Who? Where?" she said, mesmerized. It's hard work to watch someone as active as Skag McGee.

"Pete! Over there!" I pointed, and, as luck would have it, Pete looked at me at just that moment. He smiled and waved.

"He *is* cute," Gena said, sounding somewhat amazed. I don't know what she expected.

I smiled back at him, and he started working his way up the bleachers toward us. "Omigod, Gena! He's coming up here!"

111

11

PUCK: *Here she comes, curst and sad.*
Cupid is a knavish lad,
Thus to make poor females mad.

Act III, sc. ii, ll. 439–441

I imagined the meeting with Pete as a scene from a Tender Moments romance, the human drama unfolding in soap opera style right before my very eyes.

The camera zooms in on my face, my eyes shifting nervously as I am both suspicious of my best friend's intentions and anxious about my new appearance. I wave awkwardly to Pete and my lip twitches. Then the camera flashes to the dazzling Gena, calm and self-confident, innately good and hopelessly sweet. She gives a small, alluring wave. The tall, darkly handsome Pete returns a lopsided grin and waves at us. It is taking him an extraordinarily long time to scale the bleachers. He finally arrives, and to my horror the scene in my mind ends as he goes directly to Gena, completely disregarding my presence.

I felt myself begin to breathe again as Pete arrived

in real life and *Gena* was the one he overlooked. After all, he hadn't ever met her. I couldn't even think properly these days.

"Hi," he said, smiling. "I almost didn't recognize you, Skeeter. You look different."

Gena gave me an I-told-you-so look. She was still basking in the glory of having made me look cute. "I should hope so," I replied smartly. "The last time you saw me I was freezing, standing in the dark, and listening to Magic Lancaster down there." I gestured toward the court below.

Pete laughed. "Can I sit here?" he asked, pointing to the spot next to me.

"Sure," I said, and tried not to sound as wildly excited as I was. "This is my friend, Gena Farragut."

Gena smiled, said a quick hi, and went back to her vigil.

Pete glanced at the scoreboard. It read 45–43, Queen Anne leading. "Looks like it's been a good game," he said eagerly and leaned forward, his elbows on his knees.

My heart sank. He actually wanted to watch the game.

"Yeah, I guess so," I said in a low voice.

He turned toward me momentarily. "Where's your school spirit?" he joked, his face close to mine.

I glanced down at Melissa, who was in the middle of a torturous, back-bending leap. Pete looked also.

"Let's just put it this way. I don't want to risk rupturing something."

113

"I see what you mean," he said, and chuckled. "Some people really get into it."

"Like Campbell. He hasn't always been like, well, like he is now."

Pete turned toward me again, and I was very aware that our shoulders were touching. "You've known him for a long time?" he asked seriously.

I nodded. "Since preschool. My mother says we played together with the Play-Doh almost every day."

Peter guffawed. "So what are you interested in now? Or are you still into Play-Doh?"

I wanted to tell him about my writing ambitions and my love for Shakespeare, but I didn't want to turn him off by sounding like an egghead, as Shag so lovingly puts it.

Finally I grinned and said, "Promise not to laugh?"

"No." He grinned back.

"Pete!" I cried in mock exasperation. "I don't want you to get the wrong idea about what kind of girl I am."

I felt my face flushing red when I realized what I had said. I was doing that a lot lately.

"Oh, *really*," Pete said with raised eyebrows. "What kind of girl *are* you?"

"Sometimes I guess I really don't know that for sure myself . . ."

"Oh, I think I've already got some ideas about what kind of person you are," he said earnestly, as if

114

he meant it as a compliment. "Seriously, I really do want to know what you're interested in."

"I want to be a writer," I blurted out. "And I love to read Shakespeare's plays." I grimaced, but there was no laugh.

"I read *Romeo and Juliet* last year in school. It was pretty good," Pete said.

"Have you read any of his comedies?"

"No. *Romeo and Juliet* is all, and it isn't exactly a barrel of laughs."

"You've got to read this one I'm reading now!" I exclaimed. "It's called *A Midsummer-Night's Dream*, and you would *love* it."

"I would?" he said, grinning again.

"Yes. I think you would."

I explained all about Ms. Masanga's class and the funny things in the play, and Pete watched me the entire time. A couple of times, all the people around us sprang to their feet to cheer, and I was vaguely aware of the band booming in the background, but Pete's eyes never left my face, and I never quit talking.

When I finished describing the last scene I'd read, where both guys, Lysander and Demetrius, are in love with Helena, Pete said, "I'm sure glad that real life isn't so complicated."

I laughed. And then I suddenly remembered Gena. What about Gena? I had been so involved with talking to Pete, I had completely ignored her. I turned to apologize, but she was so glued to the basketball game, she didn't even know I was there.

Pete looked over at Gena's rapt expression, and then he looked puzzled. I knew what he must be thinking, because Gena didn't cheer or give the slightest indication that she knew what was going on down on the court.

"What's with your friend?" he asked. "Is she on drugs, or what?"

I had to laugh, because Gena did look pretty spaced out. "Worse than that," I responded. "She's in love with my brother, Shag. He's the school photographer, and she's watching him. There he is." I pointed at Shag, who was kneeling under the basket, aiming his camera at Campbell as he jumped to the basket.

"The guy with the red hair?"

"Yeah, that's him. Unfortunately." I glanced over at Gena to be sure she hadn't heard me. I had said enough offensive things about Shag already to strain our friendship justifiably. Thankfully, she hadn't heard.

"If your friend is so hung up on him, he can't be all bad," Pete said, noticing Gena again. "I mean, she doesn't look like the type to go out with a loser."

"Normally, you're right. But she *is* here with Campbell tonight." I raised my eyebrows as if to say "Need I say more?" Then I added, "Besides, Shag puts on an act when he's around her. He turns into a nice guy."

116

Pete laughed. "You've got it all figured out, haven't you, Skeeter?"

"If by *all* you mean Shag McGee, yes, I do." The words echoed in my head, and I realized how smug they'd sounded.

Then Pete said a strange thing. "I suppose that the people you have totally figured out never surprise you."

It was the kind of statement-question that left me wondering how to respond. I stared at him blankly, and he looked back at the game. I decided to side-step the issue.

"I've talked about *me* practically the whole game," I said. "I hardly know anything about *you.*"

Just then the final buzzer went off; Queen Anne had lost, 56–60. Gena tuned me in again, since Shag had gone off somewhere with the team.

"Too bad," she said lightly. "Ready to go?"

I looked back at Pete, who had never responded to my question. He had kept his eyes on the court. Now he turned to me and laid his hand on mine, sending an electric shiver through my body. "We'll talk about me some other time, Skeeter."

"Aren't you coming to the dance?" I knew disappointment was written all over my face. But I didn't care. I didn't want to play games with him. I didn't know how to play those kinds of games, anyway.

"No, I don't think so. I'm really glad that I saw you, though. I enjoyed our talk."

117

"Me, too."

"Well, see ya," he said.

"Okay. See ya." I thought of Juliet's first farewell to Romeo. She had put it so beautifully and full of feeling: "Good night, good night! Parting is such sweet sorrow, that I shall say good night till it be morrow." A far cry from "See ya."

A couple of guys Gena knew came up and started talking to us, and when I looked at Pete again, he had already worked his way far down the bleachers. I had an overwhelming urge to go home. As far as I was concerned, my reason for staying was gone. And I remembered, I had only two days left until the dinner party with Terry and Campbell! I had plenty of brooding to do.

But Gena's evening was just beginning. She finished her conversation with the two admirers and turned in time to catch me regretfully watching Pete leave.

"He's new, Skeeter," she said in a consoling voice. "He probably would feel really weird at the dance, not knowing anyone but you and Campbell."

"Why would it be so impossible for him to have fun with just me?" I said defensively.

"It wouldn't be," she admitted patiently. "But you shouldn't take it so personally. There could be a hundred reasons he had to leave."

"Name one."

"Skeeter! *I don't know,*" she said, growing exasperated. "You said he was moving into a new apartment. Maybe he's got a lot of unpacking to do."

"At nine-thirty at night? I don't think so."

"Look, he talked with you the entire time he was here. That must mean something."

"I didn't think you noticed."

"I noticed. You talked about that dumb play the whole time." Gena rolled her eyes in exaggerated disbelief.

"He was interested," I protested.

"I know he was," she said quickly. "That's my point exactly. I even heard him say that he'd talk with you some other time. Those were his exact words. *Some other time.* So what are you worried about? You should be thrilled!"

I smiled and started to blush. The warmth of those words — "We'll talk about me some other time, Skeeter" — flooded me. I let them tumble around in my mind, and they made me feel better and better.

Finally I giggled. "For someone who was in such a hypnotic trance watching the every movement of a certain photographer, you heard a lot of Pete's and my conversation. *Exactly,* too."

Gena smiled and seized my hand. "Come on, let's get to that dance!"

"I'm coming!" I stumbled over the bleachers trying to keep up with Gena and followed her through the crowd, out of the gym, and into the breezeway leading to the cafeteria.

The cold air felt good after the closeness of the gym and the crowd. I could see people at the end of the breezeway pushing their way into the cafeteria. The music hadn't started yet.

"Let's stop by the rest room," Gena suggested. "I want to fix my makeup." We watched a horde of girls flock past us and into the girls' restroom in the cafeteria lobby. "Let's use the one in the locker room. I bet it's empty."

"I bet it's also locked."

Gena shrugged. "It's worth a try."

"Okay." Anything, I thought, but going to the dance where I won't have anybody to dance with. Anybody, that is, whom I want to dance with.

We walked back to the gym, across the basketball court, where the referees were still talking, and into the hallway that led to the locker rooms. A few mournful players were hanging around with some of their friends.

And then I saw them. At the end of the hall, in front of the boys' locker room door, stood Shag and Pete. They had their heads together and were busy in conversation.

"Look, there's Pete and Shag," I said to Gena in a low voice and pointed.

"I didn't know they knew each other," she commented.

"They don't. Shag must be up to something."

She turned to me, fire in her eyes. "How could Shag be up to *anything?*" she shot at me. "Give him a break, Skeeter. He couldn't possibly know that you like Pete, and even if he did, what are you afraid of?

That he'll tell Pete you have leprosy? Why can't you just believe that Pete is interested in you and leave Shag out of it?"

When she put it like that, what could I say? She was right. I was being stupid and paranoid. It must be the effect of those romances, again, full of idle delusions. I pushed ahead of her and checked the girls' locker room door.

"Locked," I said.

"Yeah. We'll have to go back." Then we both looked up and watched Shag and Pete disappear into the boys' locker room. "I hope you're not mad at me," Gena said softly.

"I was hoping the same thing about you," I said in return, and smiled.

"Good. Now let's go have a good time. Okay?"

"Right."

"You first." She held the door for me.

"Let's go foot it!" I said, remembering what Juliet's father had said at his party.

Gena looked at me as if I had lost my mind, then laughed. "Whatever you say!"

12

HELENA: *O weary night, O long and tedious night,*
Abate thy hours! Shine, comforts, from the east,
That I may back to Athens by daylight,
From these that my poor company detest.

Act III, sc. ii, ll. 431–434

Campbell was already in the cafeteria when we got there, gulping a Coke and looking for Gena.

When he spotted us, he came trotting over, a huge grin on his face. "Hi!" he shouted to Gena. "You look great!"

Typical, I thought. I don't even exist.

"Thanks," Gena said. "I'm sorry we lost the game."

Campbell shrugged. "Yeah, but at least *I* had a good night! Five baskets is the best I've done in a game."

"Congratulations, Kareem," I said.

"Hi, Little Skeeter. I saw you sitting up there with Pete." He popped his eyebrows up and down in a suggestive manner.

"Yeah, Campbell. I noticed how you seemed to be aware of so much more than just what was happening on the court." I was thinking of his blatant attentions to Melissa.

Campbell gave me a puzzled look. Just then Melissa came bouncing by and joined our little group.

"Hi, you guys!" she bubbled. Her face was as red as the Christmas streamers hanging from the ceiling.

"Speak of the devil," I murmured, but only Gena acknowledged me, with an impish grin.

"*Great* game, Campbell! I mean, really GREAT! You really know how to handle that ball."

"Thanks, Melissa! Your cheers were great, too!"

Gena looked at me and rolled her eyes.

"Welcome to the mutual admiration society," I said in a loud whisper to Gena.

Campbell and Melissa either didn't hear that remark or chose to ignore it. They continued to congratulate each other with meaningless superlatives. It was revolting. Gena and I were quite relieved when Melissa was whisked away by a pack of giggling groupies.

"Hey, Gena, the band's starting now," Campbell said. "Wanna dance?"

"Okay," she said with a deadpan expression. She wasn't exactly champing at the bit. "Let me take my boots off first. Bye, Skeeter."

The happy couple plodded away. I looked around

123

the crowded cafeteria for Shag, but he wasn't anywhere to be seen. I wondered if he was still with Pete.

"Looking for someone?" Andy Walvatni said, smiling through his face of freckles.

"Oh, hi, Andy. Eaten any good chocolate lately?"

"As a matter of fact, my mom made some decent chocolate chip cookies this afternoon. I brought some for you. They're in my coat, if you're interested." Andy nodded toward the water fountain, where his coat was, I guess, but all I saw was Denny DePew leaning against the Coke machine. He hadn't changed his shirt from this afternoon.

"Thanks. Maybe later." I noticed Shag coming into the cafeteria. He was alone.

"You look nice tonight, Skeeter," Andy said, blushing.

"Thanks. So do you."

"So, would you like to dance?"

"Sure. Just as long as we end up next to those cookies."

Andy laughed. "Deal," he said, and grabbed my hand. The first dance was fast, as usual, and Andy turned out to be a pretty good dancer. I noticed Campbell and Gena dancing near us. Campbell was doing his best to convince everyone that he was really Michael Jackson, and Gena was doing her best to ignore him.

When the song was over, Andy and I headed for the cookies. Campbell was already at the table, quaffing another Coke. I decided it was now or never. I had to talk to him about being my boyfriend at the dinner party, whether I could stand the thought or not.

"Hi, again!" he shouted. The cafeteria was getting very noisy.

"Can I talk to you for a minute? Privately?"

"Anything for you," he said, bowing to me. "I'm at your service."

"Outside."

I worked my way through the crowd and out into the breezeway. Roger Patillo was leaning against a pole, talking with a couple of his friends. When I passed them, I almost choked in the smog of alcohol.

"Hiya, Skeeter," he grunted.

"Hi, Roger," I said, surprised he recognized me in his condition.

Campbell followed me down the breezeway to a quiet spot. "What's on your mind?" he asked, and rubbed his arms. "Jeez, it's *freezing* out here."

I explained the latest development of the dinner party with his family, Gena's family, and Terry's family. And then I tried to explain to him about how he should act.

"Look, you don't have to overdo it, Campbell. Just act, uh, well, *affectionate* toward me a couple of times when Terry's around. That's all."

"How do you mean?" Campbell asked with a leer. "You'll have to *show* me what you want me to do."

"Campbell, you know perfectly well what a boy-

125

friend is supposed to do!" I said loudly. Too loudly.

Roger looked over at us with a lecherous grin. "Gofer it, Campbell!" he slurred.

"Shut up, Roger," I said. He and his friends laughed.

"Really, Skeeter," Campbell insisted. "I still don't know how far you want me to go. I mean, *what do you want?* Kissing, fondling, embracing, petting?"

Roger howled and said, "Take 'em all, Skeeter!"

"ROGER, DON'T YOU HAVE ANYTHING ELSE TO DO?" I shouted.

"Oh, I get it," Roger said. "You guys need some space to be alone! Got it. See ya later!"

When they were gone, I turned back to Campbell. "Just hold my hand, and maybe put your arm around me," I said, clenching my teeth. "But *try* to do it only when Terry's around."

"Okay. You got it. Handholding and a little hugging."

"Thanks," I said, relieved, and then I thought of one last humiliating thing. "Oh, and I made up some stuff about specific dates we had, so just go along with anything she mentions to you. Okay?"

"Well, I don't know . . . What *exactly* did we do?"

"LAY OFF, CAMPBELL."

"Okay, okay," he said, grinning. "Hey, can I go back now, Lover? It's freezing out here." He laughed and strode back toward the cafeteria.

It was much colder out than when we had left for

the game, and the sky had clouded over. It felt like snow was in the air.

When I got back to the cafeteria, I wasn't surprised to see Gena dancing a slow dance with Shag and Campbell hanging all over Melissa. I made my way back to Andy and the cookies.

The rest of the evening was spent pretty much in those postures, with Gena and Shag growing ever more close and Campbell and Melissa teasing each other to the point that I feared they would break into a rousing game of tag, like fifth-graders on the playground. As William put it: "Over hill, over dale, Thorough bush, thorough brier, Over park, over pale, Thorough flood, thorough fire." Bully Bottom was in hot pursuit of fair Melissa, and she was loving every minute of the chase.

Andy and I talked about everything from his dog, which had a miserable case of fleas, to what we wanted for Christmas. He wanted a new bike or a supremely sophisticated skateboard. I told him that I wasn't absolutely positive what I wanted, but that books and a new bedroom rug were high on the list. By the time I said good-bye to Andy, I realized that he was a nice enough guy, but I knew that we didn't have a serious future together.

When Gena, Shag, Campbell, and I left, the air was so cold that Shag deemed it necessary to put his arm around Gena and hug her tightly under his jacket. Campbell didn't seem to mind that his date had been usurped. He took it rather philosophically and even made a joke of it. Or at least I thought it was a joke.

"That's what I like about dances," he announced with a broad grin. "People show their true feelings. I mean, how was I supposed to know Melissa had a crush on me all along?"

"Really," I agreed, and Gena and I grinned at each other. "You can't be expected to read people's minds."

"You got it," he said enthusiastically, puffing up his chest and jamming his hands into his pockets. Then he glanced over at Gena and Shag and said in a wistful, bittersweet voice, "Easy come, easy go."

All the way to Campbell's apartment, he explained to us why Queen Anne lost the game. I was the only one listening, since Shag and Gena were murmuring to each other in the front seat and I was stuck in the back with the jock. According to him, it was a combination of the poor timing of a couple of teammates, whose names he was too much of a sport to divulge, and the incredible ineptitude of the referees.

I breathed a sigh of relief when Shag pulled up to the ugly apartment building and Campbell piled out, but not before saying, "Thanks! See ya Sunday at your place!" and giving me a furtive wink. I averted my eyes quickly, afraid that I might lose control, and then bade him a cool "Good night." As

128

we pulled away, I looked up at the lighted windows of the building and wondered which one was Pete's.

It wasn't very far to Gena's, thank heavens, because all I did was twiddle my thumbs in the back seat, feeling like a third wheel, while Gena giggled at the witty whisperings of my brother. The Farraguts' porch light was on when we finally arrived, and Shag walked Gena to the door. I should have looked away, but wild curiosity made me watch as Shag held Gena's chin up and kissed her lightly. Just *watching* it made me feel tingly all over.

I noticed the living room curtains rustle, and then the porch light blinked. Good ole Mrs. Farragut, at it again. I could feel Gena's embarrassment. They kissed once more, and Gena went in.

Shag was silent the rest of the way home. I imagined that the feeling after kissing someone was like the feeling I had after I read the juiciest kissing scene in one of my romances. I just want to sit there awhile, remembering the events over and over again and experiencing the feelings. I thought that was probably what Shag was doing, and since I'm not completely heartless, I didn't brutally invade his reverie with such pressing issues as what he had been doing with Pete earlier in the evening.

When we got home, Mom and Dad were already in bed. I hoped Dad was feeling better. Shag had behaved acceptably, almost nobly, toward my best friend, so I felt I could afford to be charitable to him.

I said, "Good night. And thanks for the ride."

"Sure," he said kindly. "Sorry it wasn't more fun for you." And he disappeared into his room.

I wondered what he meant, since as far as he knew, I had had a fine time. Did he somehow sense that I wished Pete had stayed for the dance? I snuggled down into my bed with Romeo and started a lovely dream about Pete.

13

PUCK: *And the country proverb known,*
That every man should take his own,
In your waking shall be shown.
    Jack shall have Jill;
    Nought shall go ill;
The man shall have his mare again,
and all shall be well.

Act III, sc. ii, ll. 458–463

"*P*lease make a tossed salad, Skeeter," Mom said on Sunday afternoon. "And after that, you can make a veggie plate for appetizers."

"What's Shag doing?" I asked belligerently.

"He's chopping more wood for the fire tonight," she said, and smiled. She had been in a *very* good mood since she and Dad had had a long talk in their bedroom yesterday. "I'm sure that Shag would be more than willing to exchange jobs with you if you asked him."

"Thanks, but no thanks," I said, scowling, and headed for the refrigerator. It had snowed lightly throughout the day before and was freezing outside. There was a fresh, white, three-inch blanket over every house, lawn, and bush, and the snow was still coming. The buses were running erratically, since

131

the streets were icy, and the newscasts were warning Seattleites to stay indoors and off the roads, if possible.

Some little kids were still out playing in the snow, but most everyone else was inside keeping warm and trying to figure out how to do their Christmas shopping by telephone. The last weekend before Christmas wasn't the most convenient time to have a paralyzing snowstorm.

Mom started humming "Deck the Halls" as she rolled out the crust for a pumpkin pie.

"You're sure in a good mood," I remarked as I washed the lettuce. "Is it Christmas or the snow?"

"Neither," she said, and gave me a mysterious look. "When Shag comes in, your father and I have an announcement to make."

"Why can't you tell me now?"

"I could, but we thought it would be nice to discuss it as a family."

"*Moth-er.* Come on. I won't tell. And besides, you know how I hate secrets!" I was thinking that she was pregnant, because she had been so excited about Mrs. Lancaster's baby. And pregnancy was definitely a thing that women should talk about with each other.

Shag opened the back door and staggered in with a load of wood. "Here's your wood, lady," he said, trying to be funny. He was in a good mood, too, probably because Gena was coming over. "Where do you want it?"

"In the barrel by the fireplace, please. And be careful not to drop pieces of dirt or bark on the rug. I just vacuumed."

"Jeez, lady, do ya want the moon, or what?" Shag wisecracked.

Mom laughed. "Nope. Just no earth."

It was torture to be around such cheerfulness, and since I had finished the salad, I stuck it in the refrigerator, announced that I would do the vegetables later, and escaped to my bedroom.

Even Shakespeare seemed unusually merry, his lips twitching ever so slightly into a playful grin.

"What's so funny?" I demanded angrily. "Everything is so screwed up, how can you possibly find anything to smile about?"

Since his expression didn't change, I turned my back to him. I didn't feel like the carefree frivolity of *Someday My Prince*, my current romance, so I decided to call Gena. She, at least, would understand my pain.

I used the phone in Mom's and Dad's room. "How's it goin'?" I asked when Gena answered.

"Okay."

"Only three more hours 'til disaster."

"Uh-huh."

She must not have heard me, I thought. "Gena! Only three more hours!"

"Yeah, three more hours. How's Shag?"

My heart sank. Was this all she would ever want to talk about with me? "He's just the same as he was yesterday when you talked with him on the phone for an hour."

"Yeah, lucky me, Mom wasn't home. Hey, Skeeter, I'm *really* looking forward to this party tonight."

"I see that," I said bitterly. I would have thought that Gena might be a little more considerate of my feelings and not have kept harping on her own happiness.

"Oh, don't sound so depressed. Things aren't nearly so bad as you think."

"How can you say that?" I roared. "You know the situation. Terry is going to be here, and so is Campbell!"

"I know, I know. I just don't think you should worry about it." And then she added, with a decidedly mysterious quality to her voice, "Let's just wait and see what happens, okay?"

"Sure," I said in disgust. "Whatever you say. Good-bye."

I hung up just as Mom came into the bedroom and told me that it was time for the announcement and would I please come downstairs.

Shag sat at the kitchen table drinking a Coke. When he saw me, he winked and toasted me in a most un-Shag-like manner: "To my sister, Skeeter! May she find love and happiness this Christmas season!"

I glowered at him. "Like you have, I suppose," I said.

134

Shag just smiled.

During our little exchange, Mom and Dad had gotten a bottle of champagne out of the refrigerator and set four glasses on the table, all the while grinning like a couple of Cheshire cats.

Dad filled each glass half full.

"Isn't it a little early to be hitting the sauce, Dad?" Shag joked.

"Not in this case," Dad announced proudly. "We're celebrating the new McGee Family Nursery, which will be opening in a couple of weeks."

"You're buying the nursery?" Shag said.

"Not buying," Mom corrected. "Bought. It's a *fait accompli.*"

"Already?" I asked.

They nodded.

"When?"

"Last night. When you thought we went Christmas shopping," Mom said.

"Actually, we did go Christmas shopping," Dad said. "This is our present to each other."

They looked lovingly into each other's eyes and clinked their glasses together. Then they turned to Shag and me, and we carefully clinked their glasses.

"Congratulations," Shag said, beaming.

"Well, we've signed the papers, but the money still has to be transferred," Dad explained.

"No more headaches!" Mom exclaimed. "Dad gave his notice and will be free in two weeks."

"Hopefully, running a business won't be as stressful as my old job," Dad said calmly. "And then, theoretically, the migraines will disappear."

"They will," I said, and sipped my champagne. "I'm sure of it. I can tell that you're more relaxed already."

"And speaking of relaxed," Mom said as she gave me her get-with-it look, "I think you've relaxed enough this afternoon, young lady. Make that veggie plate and set out the dishes of peanuts, chips, and dip. Shag, you put the leaf in the table and set it. For *twelve*. Our guests will be arriving soon."

The Farraguts were the first to arrive. Shag answered the door because I was afraid it might be Terry. Gena looked absolutely ravishing, wearing a blue silk blouse and soft gray slacks and with her hair in a single braid. Shag took her coat, and Dad, who had arrived on the scene soon after Shag, took Mrs. Farragut's coat and Hilary's ski jacket.

"I brought my *Black Stallion* report for you to see, Skeeter," Hilary said, producing a blue folder that she had protected under her coat. "I got an A."

"Great. I'll read it later, okay?"

"Okay."

"It's *still* snowing," Mrs. Farragut complained, and she fluffed her hair. She looked right at me and didn't mention the Safeway incident, so I hoped she had dismissed it as teenage craziness.

"This is for you," she said, handing a box of expensive Frango chocolate mints to my mother, who

136

had appeared in the kitchen doorway. "Merry Christmas."

"Thank you!" Mom said. "They'll be perfect after-dinner treats."

Shag offered to get everyone a drink, and, predictably, Gena offered to assist him in his arduous task. I wondered if I'd ever have a private conversation with her again. It would never occur at my house, that much was certain. I felt even sadder at the prospect, because it made me feel more lonely and that much more anxious about keeping Terry's friendship.

Dad didn't know Mrs. Farragut very well, but he managed to strike up a conversation with her quite quickly. Business people speak a strange language, I thought, as I listened to them.

"So, are you bullish or bearish now, Diana?"

"Definitely bullish. It's a bull market. I'm buying."

"Anything in particular?"

"Oh, mainly blue chips."

Bull chips, I thought. It would be more interesting to talk to Hilary.

Hilary was explaining to me about how she had drawn a different character from the story on each page of the report when the doorbell buzzed again. I cringed, realizing that I was the only McGee nearby and available for greeting guests. I opened the door and let the Lancasters in.

"Hiya, babe!" Campbell blurted out, before I had a chance to tell him that Terry hadn't arrived yet. "You look *sensational*, as always!" Then he reached down and hugged me.

Mr. and Mrs. Lancaster looked just as startled as I must have.

"Hi, Campbell," I said, tight-lipped. "*Not everyone is here yet*, so just make yourself comfortable and Shag will get you something to drink."

"Oh, I get it," Campbell said in a low voice as he passed me on the way to the kitchen.

"Good." I turned back to Mr. and Mrs. Lancaster, who still looked rather astonished. "I'll take your coats. It's still snowing, I see!"

"Yes, it certainly is," Mrs. Lancaster said, struggling out of her coat. She was huge. It was hard to believe she still had another whole month to go.

"Here's some eggnog, made especially for this occasion," Mr. Lancaster announced.

"No rum for you, Annie!" Dad called from the front room.

"Of course not, Dr. McGee!" Mrs. Lancaster said, and laughed. "Is your mom in the kitchen, Skeeter?"

"Yes. Mrs. Lancaster, do you know Mrs. Farragut and Hilary Farragut?"

"No, I don't think so," she said, and smiled sweetly at Hilary. "Hi, Hilary."

"Hi," Hilary said very quietly. She was shy around grownups.

Dad took care of the adult introductions, and Mrs.

138

Lancaster went into the kitchen and Mr. Lancaster went into the front room. Hilary and I were alone again. Alone with the *Black Stallion* report, that is.

Finally the doorbell buzzed, and I knew the moment of truth had come. Terry was here. Campbell heard the doorbell and bounded into the hallway, placing his arm around me as I opened the door.

"Hi, Skeeter. I'm Terry, and this is my father, David Peat."

I couldn't believe my eyes.

14

THESEUS: *Here come the lovers, full of joy and mirth.*
Joy, gentle friends! joy and fresh days of love
Accompany your hearts!

Act V, sc. i, ll. 28–30

*T*erry, my pen pal of two years — the one person who knew about my Raptures and Tender Moments and the embarrassing details of my nonexistent dates with Campbell — was none other than Pete, my handsome Romeo.

"I don't believe this," I moaned.

"Oh, man!" Campbell shouted, dropping his arm from my shoulder. "*You!* You're Skeeter's Terry?"

"I hope so," Pete said softly, staring at me. "I hope you're not angry, Skeeter."

I was speechless, and I stood there for what seemed a very long time, staring back at Pete — or rather Terry — as understanding seeped slowly into my brain.

Mom came out of the kitchen, followed by Gena, Shag, and Mrs. Lancaster. "For goodness' sake,

140

Skeeter! Invite the Peats in!" she said in a very perturbed voice.

I stepped back so Mom and the rest of the world could meet Terry Rothschild Peat and his famous father. Mom looked quite astonished, but she didn't miss a beat in conducting the introductions, a task I was too stupefied to handle myself.

Pete, I mean *Terry*, was as handsome as ever. And the resemblance between father and son was remarkable — the same hair, the same eyes, Terry with his deep dimples, Mr. Peat with his chin. The only thing missing on Terry was the glasses.

I should have known, I thought. I *should* have. Friday night, at the game, he was so easy to talk to, it was like we had been old friends. I remembered his remark about me: "I suppose that the people you have totally figured out never surprise you." Why didn't he tell me *then? Why didn't he tell me two years ago!* I began to feel deceived and angry. He had had plenty of opportunities to let me know the truth, and he didn't. He led me on and made me look like a fool.

Mom finished the introductions. "Now that everyone knows each other," she said happily, "make yourselves at home. Dinner will be ready soon." She took the bottle of wine that Mr. Peat handed her and thanked him.

Dad invited Mr. Peat into the front room, where he, Mr. Lancaster, and Mrs. Farragut had been talking. Mom and Mrs. Lancaster retreated to the kitchen with Hilary, who volunteered to whip the potatoes. And Gena, Shag, Campbell, Terry, and I were left standing in the hallway.

Shag sank down on the stairs, a smug look on his face. "The expression on your face was absolutely priceless, Skeeter," he said and laughed.

"Shag!" Gena chided. "Be nice."

"*You knew?*" I asked Shag. I was incredulous.

He just smiled and glanced over at Terry.

"I told him after the game on Friday," Terry said to me, looking very guilty. "I needed some information from him."

"You're a louse and a fraud, Terry Peat," I said angrily. "And I'm not the least bit surprised that you're in league with the likes of Shag."

Gena frowned. "Don't be so hard on Terry, Skeeter," she said. "He meant to tell you when he first got to Seattle."

"How do *you* know that?" I asked, confused.

And then it dawned on me. Shag must have told her yesterday during their marathon phone conversation. I wondered if everyone had known about Terry except me. And the very thought made me even more furious.

Gena looked sheepish.

"Oh, I see," I said, and gave her a dirty look. "And I suppose you knew about this big joke, too, didn't you, Campbell?"

He grinned stupidly. "I didn't know anything!" he boasted.

"Skeeter," Terry said, "Gena's right. I meant to tell you."

"Oh, really?" I said sarcastically. "Who was stopping you?"

"Remember that day when I met you and Campbell outside the apartment building?"

I nodded.

"Campbell knew my name was Terry, but he's used to calling guys by their last names, so he called me Peat. You thought he meant Pete, P-E-T-E, and before I could tell you my full name, he introduced you and then I knew who you really were. You had said in your letters that Campbell was your boyfriend, but it didn't look to me like you two were very tight. You had been giving him a pretty dirty look before I said hello. Frankly, Skeeter, I didn't want to embarrass you."

Campbell hooted. "Oh, wow, this is great! I was supposed to act like Skeeter's boyfriend tonight. Right, Skeeter?"

"Shut up, Campbell."

"It looks like there's more than one pretender here," Shag observed with a patronizing air. "You're both liars."

Gena giggled. "Shag," she crooned, "you don't have to be so blunt."

"Why not? They're a couple of fakes putting on an act for each other. I'm just calling it like I see it."

"As long as we're calling people like we see them . . ." I began, glaring at Shag.

Just then Hilary peeped out at us from the kitchen door. "Dinner's ready," she announced, and blushed. I remembered how it felt to be a ten-year-old in the presence of cute, older guys.

"All *right!*" Campbell shouted. "I'm so hungry I could eat a horse."

Hilary looked stricken. "You do," she warned, "and you're a goner."

The snow was falling much faster now, in flakes the size of half-dollars. Everything was very cozy, with the fire and the delicious dinner on the table, but I was too upset to feel properly festive.

Dad filled the adults' wineglasses. Shag, who sat at the end of the table with Gena, held up his milk glass to be filled.

"I think you've had your share with the champagne earlier," Dad remarked.

"I can handle it," Shag said, smiling at Gena.

"I'm sure you could," Dad countered with a grin, and passed by him.

Mrs. Farragut, who was sitting to my right, sniffed her wine. "This has a lovely bouquet, David. Is it a Chardonnay?"

"Why, yes it is," Mr. Peat said, and nodded. He was strategically seated on the other side of Mrs. Farragut. Probably my mother's doing. "Do you know wines?"

"Not really," she said, blushing. "It was just a lucky guess."

"You're too modest."

144

I tuned them out and shifted my attention to the conversation across the table. I was doing my best to ignore Terry, who sat on the other side of me. Mom was telling Mrs. Lancaster the reason for the champagne and how excited she was about the new business. Mrs. Lancaster was trying to listen to all of the boring intricacies of the business deal as Mom recounted them, but she was obviously uncomfortable. She kept shifting in her chair and pressing her sides.

"Are you all right, Annie?" Mom finally asked.

"Oh, I'm fine. It's probably just heartburn, and I did have a busy day today. I started unpacking the kitchen dishes."

"You shouldn't be doing that!" Mom scolded. "I'll come over bright and early tomorrow to help."

I heard Dad asking Mr. Lancaster about the best computer system for the new business, and, at the far end of the table, Campbell and Hilary had their heads together, talking about who knows what.

In fact, everyone was having a good time, laughing, complimenting Mom and the food, and chatting merrily away. Everyone, that is, except Terry and me.

My mind kept flitting back to countless embarrassing things I had put in my letters. I had actually recommended my favorite Tender Moments romances to him. I wondered if he had laughed hysterically when he read those letters. And the dates with Campbell that I had described in sordid detail! Every time I tried to say something to Terry, one of

145

those letters would pop into my mind and choke back my words. It was all so humiliating, so extremely humiliating.

Finally, the silence between us was unbearable. "Why didn't you tell me two years ago, when I first wrote to you?" I spit out in a low voice. "You knew I thought you were a girl."

"Yeah, I knew," he said.

And then I thought of something else. "You even told me that you got a permanent, and that you got pimples during your, well," I said, lowering my voice to the quietest possible whisper, *"your time of the month!"*

"I *did* experiment with a permanent a long time ago," he said defensively, "and I hated it. And as for the pimples bit, I just said that I was going to a dermatologist every month because of my acne."

I felt terribly stupid for a moment, and then I recouped. Maybe I did assume it was that-time-of-the-month pimples, but I wasn't going to let him off the hook that easily. "You led me on," I accused.

Terry was silent.

"And another thing. Do you really play volleyball?" I paused and thought of something else. "And where did you get all of that pastel stationery?"

"Yes, I really play volleyball," he said, annoyed. "I learned when I was in Hawaii one summer. And as for the stationery, I found it in our desk drawer at home. I wasn't trying to be *that* sneaky!"

I looked away. Maybe he didn't plan every deception, but the fact remained that he *had* deceived me. "Why did you do it?" I finally said.

"It's hard to say, exactly." He hesitated and then looked at me. Our eyes met. "I guess I wanted you to be the real you when you wrote to me. And I thought that if you knew I was a boy, you would be different."

I knew he was probably right. I probably would have been much more reserved if I'd known he was one of the opposite sex! And I certainly wouldn't have told him the things I did!

"But didn't you worry that I'd find out sooner or later?" I asked, feeling a little closer to him.

"Yeah, but I figured that it would come later, after we were already good friends." He paused and pushed his cranberry sauce around with his fork. "We've shared so much already, Skeeter. I was hoping when I moved here that we could share even more."

The warm fire across the room reflected the heat of my face. I could see the snow piling up against the front window and sitting next to Terry, I remembered the exciting touch of his hand at the game and felt the growing sense of what he wanted us to be. I was slowly beginning to believe it: Terry and Pete were the same person. A person that I not only liked as a friend but also wanted as a boyfriend.

"I guess you're still Terry, even if you are a boy." I chuckled and looked into his blue eyes.

"And you're still Skeeter, but without a boyfriend

named Campbell." He grinned and was about to say something else when Mrs. Lancaster stood up, holding her protruding abdomen.

"Excuse me, but I'm just in so much pain."

Everybody stopped talking and watched her helplessly for a moment. "Do you think you're in labor, honey?" Mr. Lancaster asked, rushing over to her.

"I think so. It's beginning to seem like regular contractions." She moaned and leaned on the back of her chair.

"But it's *too early!*" Campbell cried. His face was white and his eyes bugged out. "Get a watch! Start timing the contractions!" he yelled, his voice becoming a panicky squeal. "HOW ARE WE GOING TO GET TO THE HOSPITAL IN THIS SNOW?" Those were Campbell's last words. He fell out of his chair sideways and onto the floor with a thud. He had fainted. Campbell Lancaster, the great obstetric expert, was out cold.

Hilary flew into action. "I know what to do," she announced, and got a pillow and the afghan from the couch. "We just finished fainting in Health."

Everybody took her word for it, and all attention focused back on Mrs. Lancaster, who definitely was in labor. She closed her eyes and breathed rhythmically through her mouth. "One's starting now, Greg," she said to Mr. Lancaster, and he looked at his watch.

"I'll call the hospital!" Mom cried.

"What can I do?" Mr. Peat asked. "How about a car? Do you have any chains?" he asked my dad.

"Yes. In the garage," Dad said, heading for the kitchen. "Come on, Shag."

"I've got a set of chains, too," Mrs. Farragut said breathlessly. "Maybe we should take two cars. In case one gets stuck."

"Good idea, Diana!" David Peat exclaimed. "I'll go with you to your house to get them."

Oh no, I thought. Not those two, together. *Alone.* They can't be trusted. They might get passionately involved at Mrs. Farragut's house! And then where would Mrs. Lancaster be? My mind started racing. How to stop them from leaving together? What could I do?

Then I stopped myself. This was ridiculous, absurd. Real people don't act like Angelica Fairfield, *thank heavens.*

Still, I was relieved when Terry said, "I'll go, too! You may need help putting them on her car."

Mom came back into the dining room and reported that the hospital was expecting Mrs. Lancaster and she should leave as soon as possible. "In the meantime, come and lie down on the couch, Annie," Mom said, and she led the Lancasters into the living room.

After they had gone, only Gena, Hilary, Campbell, and I were left in the dining room. Hilary had Campbell's legs propped up, his body covered with

149

blankets and her water-soaked napkin draped across his forehead. He had regained consciousness but was still weak from the shock.

"Well," Gena sighed, "this has been quite an evening."

"You can say that again." I forgot that I had mascara on and rubbed my eyes. "This stuff makes my eyes itch," I complained.

"I know. Hey, Skeeter, I'm sorry I didn't tell you about Terry. Shag made me promise."

"It's okay," I said and smiled. "It worked out okay. Besides, I probably wouldn't have believed you anyway!"

She laughed. "Have you noticed my mom and Terry's dad?" she asked, and stretched her arm over her head, balancing herself with the back of the chair.

"Yeah. I think they like each other."

"*Like* each other? That's the understatement of the year," Gena declared.

"They just met, for heaven's sake. They're being *cordial.*" I felt proud of my newly rational attitude.

"If I know *anything* about love, and I think I do," Gena said meaningfully, "I think we are dealing with a genuine love-at-first-sight relationship here."

"I don't believe in love at first sight," I said flatly.

"Oh, really? Well let me put it in terms that you do believe in. Puck, your dear little Shakespearean cupid, dropped love juice not only in Mr. Peat's eyes, but also in Terry's."

150

"Maybe." I giggled. "Come on. Let's clear the table."

When Mr. Peat, Mrs. Farragut, and Terry returned with the Farraguts' car, Dad and Shag had Odor ready to go also. Mom and Mr. Lancaster helped Mrs. Lancaster into Odor, and they left. Mr. Lancaster assured us that they were in plenty of time, since the contractions were still fifteen minutes apart. Mrs. Lancaster looked pretty ragged, though. I was relieved when the convoy pulled away.

Mom, Shag, Terry, Gena, and I stayed home. And, of course, Campbell and Hilary. The last time I checked, Hilary was reciting her *Black Stallion* report to her captive audience of one.

Mom, Shag, and Gena decided to make some hot chocolate.

"Can we talk?" Terry asked me. "I have something I'd like to give you."

"Sure," I said nervously. I led him into the living room, where we were completely alone. All the lights were out, and the room glowed with the light from the fire. I reached to turn on a lamp, and Terry touched my hand.

"I don't think we need that," he said. "Let's just look at the fire."

"Okay," I said, and tried to swallow the lump in my throat. We sat on the couch together, side by side, the way I had dreamed about sitting with Campbell. The fire crackled, and I thought I could feel Terry's breathing on my hair.

151

"I wanted to give you a present, Skeeter," he said softly, and pulled a package out from behind him. I hadn't even noticed it. "Merry Christmas."

"Terry!" I said, surprised.

"I hope you like it," he said.

"I feel funny about accepting this, after what I called you."

"You mean 'a louse' and 'a fraud'?" He grinned.

I laughed. "Something like that."

"I've been called worse. Go ahead. Open it."

"It looks like a book."

"Yes, it does. Now, will you just open it!"

"Okay! Okay!" I ripped off the pale pink ribbon and tore off the paper. "Oh, Terry!" I gasped. "I love it." It was the old copy of *A Midsummer-Night's Dream* with Puck on the cover and gilt-edged pages that Shag had tried to sell me.

"Read the inscription," he said.

I carefully opened the cover to find a short inscription in Terry's familiar handwriting.

Dear Skeeter,
 A classic book for a classic person. I'll be your friend always.
      Love,
      Terry

I don't exactly know how or why I did what I did next, but it came very naturally. I leaned my head on Terry's shoulder and whispered, "Thank you." I

152

closed my eyes and could feel his heart beating, strong and fast, and I could smell the faint odor of cedar chips on his sweater.

I felt Terry's arm around me, and I wanted to stay like that, close to him, forever.

But Terry moved. He raised his hand from my shoulder and brushed it through my hair. "My sweet Skeeter," he said, and leaned over, gently putting his lips on mine. It was a wonderfully exciting first kiss, a kiss that told me that Terry truly cared about the real me, all of me. And that was what made it so perfect.

15

PUCK: *If we shadows have offended,*
Think but this, and all is mended,
That you have but slumb'red here
While these visions did appear.
And this weak and idle theme,
No more yielding but a dream.

Act V, sc. i, ll. 430–435

*I*t's the last Saturday night of our glorious Christmas vacation, and I'm waiting for Terry to come over. We're going to a movie. Shag is over at Gena's. She's babysitting for Hilary, so Shag rented a movie for two bucks to play on the video cassette recorder Mrs. Farragut bought for Christmas. Gena agreed to pay for the movie out of her babysitting money only if Shag paid for the treats during the movie. Gena knows how to handle my brother. She is also happy because her mother is nicer and *busier* now that she's dating Mr. Peat.

I've been a little easier on Shag lately, too, since I found out that he sold Terry the copy of *A Midsummer-Night's Dream* at cost. For Shag, that was true sacrifice.

Mrs. Lancaster had a healthy baby girl, who they

154

named Libby Lancaster. Terry laughed when I told him and asked if there was some significance in their naming both of their kids after canned foods.

"Well, William," I said, as I finished reviewing the play, "everybody ended up with whom they were supposed to, just like in my romance novels."

Shakespeare smiled, and I knew what he was thinking. "But methinks that the real thing rates much greater."

I agreed.